# THE
# CHANGING PLACE

### BY
## KRIS VILLARREAL

*"You can't go back, only forward."*
— Conrad Fink

*In memory of Conrad Fink, who gave me courage and showed me that I am deserving of all my dreams.*

# Chapter 1

# ACCIDENTS HAPPEN

I WAS ALWAYS JUST a little bit crooked—slanted to the side, without really noticing. There was a slight unevenness in the pace of my steps, a curve in my left shoulder that shot right through to my left foot, causing me to hobble along most of the time. Stumbling through life, muddling my way about the days, and trying to stay hidden was usually how I went about things.

My walk was slow and because of it, time had always mattered more to me than to other kids. I had to measure the time it would take me to get anywhere, longer than most, slower than most, and so I mapped out everything and counted my steps along the way. The truth of it is time doesn't care about you, so you'd better move your ass. Because no matter what, time always passes somehow. No matter how sad you feel, no matter how stuck you might be. Time always seems to move right along, with or without your permission.

The kids in school gave me shit for the slight limp, and

it kept me from getting into any athletics. Sports made it easy to get popular. I wasn't popular, but I wasn't hated either. Few kids gave me the time of day really, except for Trish and Liza—my only friends. It'd been the three of us for just about forever now. They put up with me, and so I put up with them. It wasn't bad being the one guy in school without any guy friends. Most guys didn't like me. A few thought I was gay, but that was a lie. If you ask me, it had more to do with the fact I was emotionally mature, and for that, they didn't understand me. But maybe some of it had to do with the limp. They had names for me: gimpy, hop-along, the limpster was probably my favorite.

Eighth grade was like a war zone. Dodging bullets, taking cover, praying for survival.

I could tell fall was growing near, although it wasn't cold out. I felt a peculiar chill in my bones. My hands were trembling, my mind shaking as I unpacked my school work for the evening. The anxiety of loneliness was crippling me, more so than the hunch in my shoulder. My uncle, my mom's brother, would be home soon. If I wasn't studying by the time he got home, he'd start some shit. I wasn't in the mood for his threats, and I couldn't take any more rants about how useless I was.

He'd never been nice. So why I expected him to suddenly swap personalities with a real human being, I wasn't sure. Despite the situation, he stayed the same—pissed. Uncle Kasey was pissed off at the world, and as for why, hell, I'm not sure, but I sure wished he'd get over it already and start living his damn life. The shit was passing him by, but he didn't care.

I sat at the kitchen table, waiting, when I heard the

dryer go off in the garage. Our kitchen was small, old, and my mom had painted the worn-out cabinets a canary yellow. She said it would make it feel like it was summer even when it wasn't. It didn't.

The whole house looked a bit tattered and run-down. It felt homey, though, cozy and warm, and the wood paneling throughout made it feel more like a cottage. Footsteps creaked on the old hardwood so you always knew when someone was coming or going. No one had done laundry in weeks, and I'd run out of underwear that could be turned inside out. I knew Warren needed clean clothes too, so I'd started a load of our clothes as soon as I got home from school.

Warren still wasn't home, but I couldn't worry about him now. My uncle would be home in less than five minutes, and Uncle Kasey didn't scream at Warren as much as he did me. Maybe he picked on me and not Warren because I was older. He expected more from me, and I never could give it. The numbness I felt helped me to evade responsibility or any sense of guilt. I pulled the clothes from the dryer, put them in the clothes hamper, and started folding. I stopped short when I heard a buzzing sound. Sitting there on top of the dryer was my mom's cell. I found it strange that no one had noticed it there, but it was still connected to the charger.

"*Message from Stuart,*" it read.

I hadn't seen my father in eleven days. Not since the night my mom died. No one knew where he was, and no one had bothered to try and find him. Not even me. Out of anger and curiosity, I grabbed the phone and read the

38 messages he'd sent since she died. And all it did was make me hate him even more.

The most recent read, "*You left me here. I can't believe you left me like this, Daisy. I've got no one now. God, someone help me.*"

How could anyone be so goddamn pathetic? Sure your wife's dead, but your kids are still here, you bastard. He gave up on this family the moment we found out about the stomach cancer. The night she died was engraved in the back of my mind. The three of us: me, Dad, and Warren sat in the waiting room outside the ER. When the doctor came out, he wrung his hands in an irritated way, as if what he were about to say was an inconvenience for him. His eyes searched for us, but he wouldn't look at our faces. It was strange, and I knew then. One glance at me, and I knew she was dead. It sat there on his face and on his lips before he even said a word. My dad had never been very intuitive, so he stood up and walked toward the doctor, and there was hope in that walk. I couldn't hear what they said, but my dad fell to his knees, sobbing.

Warren just stood there with Dad, tugging on his shirt. I stayed in the waiting room chair, my arms folded across my chest and my legs sprawled out before me. I started to chew on my fingernails, and if Mom would have been there, if Mom had stayed living for just a few more hours, she would have knocked my hand down from my mouth.

"Stop that shit, Stephen," she would have said. "Putting those dirty fingernails in your mouth." I pictured her shaking her head in disbelief.

Eleven days. Eleven days.

I missed her. But I couldn't let myself think about just how much I really missed her, because it would have left me debilitated. And whether I wanted to or not, I knew I had to hold myself together for Warren's sake. The little shit needed me.

"The fuck are you doing?" My uncle appeared at the door to the garage. I hadn't been listening for the sound of his car, and the noise from the washer-dryer had hidden the slam of our front door. His overly-rounded shadow cast upon the concrete floor of the garage. I didn't answer him, and shoved my mom's phone into my jeans pocket, turning it off as I did. "Did you fucking hear me?" he slurred. "Hey, gimpy, you better answer me when I'm talking to you."

"Sorry," I said with too much friction. I dropped my eyes and focused on folding the clothes on top of the dryer. Looking Uncle Kasey in the eyes would only end in more screaming, sometimes hitting, if he was drunk enough and pissed enough. "I'm doing some laundry. Warren ran out of clean clothes." I emphasized Warren knowing that if he thought it had been for me he'd start more shit.

"Oh," he muttered, turning and making a move toward the TV room. "Well, get your ass in here and make me some damn dinner. Where the hell is Warren anyway?" He jerked his head back, turning around to face me.

Shit, I hadn't seen that one coming. Warren hadn't said a word about where he'd been going after school, even though I'd tried twice already to trick him into telling me. My guess was that he'd rather be anywhere but here. I felt the same, but I wouldn't and couldn't admit to feeling that way. If I'd wanted to, I knew Liza and her mom would have taken me in. She lived one house down from mine, and I'd spent too much time there growing up. We were practically siblings, but not in that picturesque, loving way you see in the movies. It was more of a "you annoy the hell out of me, but I've known you too long to desert you now" type of way. But as for Warren, I think he just hated me. He was too young and dumb to realize his survival depended on my existence.

"He stayed after school." I hated lying. It made me feel even more self-conscious. It was almost as if I were standing there in front of my uncle with deflated tubes in place of my arms and legs. "Coach Miller is having him run drills. Thinks he might have a shot at something big someday. He's trying to tire the lazy out of him before he gets to high school."

"Someday? Coach said that, huh?" he paused, grinning while steadying his weight with a sloppy grip on the door frame. I hated that smile. It was meant to be malicious, a warning of things to come, but it made him look like a smirking five-year-old. The smile made my stomach jump, like a fist knocking you in the gut. "That washed up piece of shit doesn't know a motherfucking thing." I could almost hear his tongue cutting against his teeth when he said "thing." "Warren will be a goddamn hockey star. And you can tell that asshole I said so."

He slammed the door, and I heard his clunky leather work boots pounding on the weakening floors as he plopped down on our couch. I stayed in the garage, finishing all the laundry, in an attempt to avoid him. The sunlight shining through the garage window grew dimmer and dimmer, and still there was no sign of Warren. A blade of lightning struck the ground outside and lit up the dark garage. I jumped, my eyes drifting back to the door.

Warren wasn't at hockey practice. I'd heard around school that he hadn't been to practice in weeks. He'd become a total ass of late, but hockey was everything to him. It made no sense. And now I couldn't stop worrying about where the hell he could be.

Something changed in Warren when Mom died. Before she got sick, he was this sweet, eager kid—bulky for his age, and a tad bit intimidating, but that was his appeal. He used to shuffle behind me and Trish on our way home from school, bugging me with questions about comic books and the girls in his grade. He was a gentle ogre, always wanting to do the right thing, but now he was holding on to all this anger. A part of him blamed the world for what happened to Mom, and he was determined to make us all suffer for it. No small thing could go unnoticed.

In school that morning, I'd seen him harassing some sixth-grader who bumped into him in the hallway. The kid had said sorry, but that wasn't good enough for Warren. Nothing was.

He used to tell me things. We used to talk, not a lot, but still, now I was lucky if I could get a few grunts out of him. I didn't know what to do. He'd never stayed out this late before. Lake Odessa shut down at seven o'clock like all the other small towns in Michigan, like all the small towns anywhere I assumed, but I'd never been outside the Mitten.

I shifted my weight to my left foot. My right knee throbbed and swelled. I'd been bearing down on it for too long. The sharp pain brought on thoughts about my dad. Warren didn't see him leave that night. It was only me. We left the hospital, left Mom there, because we had to. And it wasn't her we left, but the shell of her. When we got home, Dad wouldn't get out of the car. He drove us there, without speaking.

And when the car pulled up to our hurried home, time stopped. We all sat there, staring at the house, afraid to go inside, afraid we would see Mom's ghost in the darkness. But she was gone now. We all knew that.

"Dad," Warren said, trying to get his attention, but he didn't respond. I unlocked my door and stepped out; Warren followed. I couldn't wait for my dad to pull himself together. Warren and I had to be at school in the morning. I unlocked the door to our house and turned on the lights in the TV room. My uncle had passed out on the couch. Warren pushed past me, heading toward his bedroom. The door slammed, and he disappeared. I stood in the front doorway, watching my dad's vacant expression. I didn't call out to him. I watched and waited, but he stayed put. Once I'd waited long enough, I went to my bedroom and fell asleep.

My dad didn't sleep in his bedroom that night. I woke in the early morning to the sound of the front door slamming. I jumped up and ran to the edge of the driveway to watch our car chase the sunrise. Without thinking, I chased after the car, running down the street barefoot, in nothing but my boxers.

"You can't leave me here!" I shouted through my short breaths. My right knee swelled then, just as it was now. "She's fucking gone too. You can't leave me here with him." I could still hear my own voice inside my head. The pain in my knee got to be too much, and I fell into the road, crying, with no one to comfort me.

I finished folding the last load of laundry and decided I couldn't prolong the inevitable. The refrigerator door had opened and closed a total of four times. My uncle couldn't be that drunk yet, unless he'd been grabbing two beers at a time.

Rain splattered and stuck to the garage window. Lightning lit up the trees in the yard across the street, while I focused on keeping my breathing even. I didn't want my uncle to sense my fear while he sat on the couch, waiting for me to come inside the house. My eyes sought the door. I needed to keep as quiet as possible. Even with the drumming of the rain and the crashing of the thunder, I could hear my uncle snoring. He *had* been grabbing two at a time. Right foot, followed by the left—eight steps total to clear the garage, and I needed to make each one softer than the last if I didn't want my face smashed in.

My survival instincts felt raw. I'd grown to be more alert, more aware of danger since living with Uncle Kasey. When it was just me, my folks, and Warren, I hadn't known danger or fear. Now, I held it in my breath as soon as I walked through my front door. Now, I knew the cracking sound that a fist made when it hit a jaw. I knew what it meant to feel like you might die from the pain of the blows, but the words cut deeper. Those bruises didn't fade. You never know what might set off someone like Uncle Kasey. I could stay quiet and he would still find something to pick at. Last Thursday, he popped me on the back of my head at dinner for chewing too loudly. He sat there cock-eyed, completely crazy, smacking his gums together, trying to emulate the way a camel eats, and looking more like a deranged hippo with a breathing disorder.

I crossed the garage in the swiftest manner possible. When I reached the door, I put my ear to the dark-blond particle wood and listened for the sound of more snoring. There was nothing. In the moment that I leaned back from the door, my uncle whipped it open and grabbed me by the collar of my t-shirt, pulling me through the door. His grip ripped the shirt. I heard it tear. He brought me close to his face. I could smell stale beer and rotting teeth as he heaved like a dog. Anyone would have switched to mouth-breathing to avoid the smell, but I refused to breathe any part of that bastard into me.

"You left the fucking porch light on," he said calmly, chest heaving. "How many fucking times do I have to tell you to turn off the goddamn porch light?" He shook me, forcing me to answer. It wasn't a question that needed an answer. Turning the porch light on when I got home from school was something I'd been doing since my mom got sick. That was when the night terrors started. The light shined through our backyard and allowed me to see between the trees to Lake Jordan whenever I had trouble sleeping. My uncle had bawled at me about the light for the first few nights he stayed with us, saying it would lead burglars and wild animals to the house. That was complete bullshit, but I didn't argue with him.

"I forgot," I stuttered. My hands grabbed at his own, trying to loosen the grip he had around my neck. I was trying to wriggle my way out, and at the sight of me struggling, the corner of his mouth lifted into a smile, yellow teeth gleaming for what seemed like only half of a second. Then his lips flashed to a satisfied frown.

"Where the hell is Warren?" he spat.

"I don't fucking know," I screamed as he pulled me off the ground. He threw me down, and I slid across the floor. My hands caught the floorboards, and I thought about running to my room and locking the door. He was drunk enough that he might not catch me.

"Don't you fucking curse at me." He kicked me in my right knee, my swollen knee. I winced, but I didn't look up at him as he towered over me, a greasy, pink hippo in a too-tight gray tank top that looked more like his own damn skin.

His feet were spread hip-width apart, and I watched as the light from the TV reflected off the metal of his steel-toe boots. This was how my uncle got his kicks—torturing the weak because he had grown bored with only torturing himself. It was impossible, it seemed, that he and my mom had come from the same home, the same parents. Why did he have to be such an asshole? It made no sense. And I'm not saying my mom had been perfect. Once, she punched another mom in the jaw after one of Warren's hockey games just because the woman complained about Warren being rough with the team. Our neighbors had whispered about her temper.

They all had known you didn't mess with Daisy Wilkes. She had been one proud lady. Uncle Kasey was ashamed of something, and I couldn't pity him. I couldn't care about him—not if he lived or died. He was a worthless piece of shit, and he would regret treating me like a vessel for his aggression. He tossed me my faded blue jean jacket, and I made no movement to try and catch it. It landed in my lap, and I looked up at my worthless uncle.

"Get the fuck out of here, and go find him. Find Warren, and bring him home."

I scrambled to get off the floor, donned the coat, and headed for the door—twelve steps.

"And turn off that goddamn porch light, you useless piece of shit!"

## CHAPTER 2

# A LIGHT IN THE CLEARING

I SLAMMED THE DOOR shut behind me and stepped onto our chipped, white porch. Moonlight filtered through the trees. Wind tousled the blood-red leaves that still lingered. The rain had stopped, but the wind beat into me. There was a cold front coming in, and the precipitation from the lake had brought down the night fog. I loved nights like this—staring out into the misty trees watching steam rise up from the water as I lay safely under the covers of my bed.

No one wanted to be outside on a night like this, not even Warren.

I buttoned up my coat to my chin and walked around the side of the house to grab my silver, three-speed bike. For me, riding was easier than walking. The bike provided more balance.

It hadn't been cold on the bike ride home from school, but now it was bitter, biting. I stood there unmoving. A part of me was afraid to wander off into the night. I was strong-willed, but I wasn't stupid. I knew I was still a kid. Fourteen isn't old enough for anything but either staying quiet or running. And unfortunately, I wasn't good at running.

Sam the Man, Warren's only friend, was a short, stocky pisser who talked a big game. He never shut up, even when it was clear no one was listening. Sam was always desperate for attention; he talked over everyone else's conversations in the cafeteria, and made up lies about a rich cousin that we knew didn't exist. I wasn't sure if Sam even really liked Warren. Warren was popular in seventh grade, and Sam clung to him for that reason. It was a friendship of convenience, but it wasn't my place to say anything.

I rode the six blocks toward the town square, which was just past Sam's street. His home was a beat-up, cream-colored ranch with pink trim. The hideous, tiny home hurt my eyes. The front yard was always unkempt, as bushes grew into the street. Sam's mom was a widow, and a bit batty. One night she wandered throughout the streets in her nightgown, screaming and shouting, not making a bit of sense. People around town whispered about her losing her mind. It embarrassed Sam, and the kids in school teased him for it. And even though I found Sam irritating, I pitied his mom. We all break down sometimes.

When I edged up to Sam's house, the lights were out. There were no cars parked in the drive. Newspapers piled up on the front doorstep. It almost looked like no one lived there, or they were just out of town and Warren hadn't mentioned it. I still thought to knock, but as I suspected, there was nothing. After that, I did what any big brother would have done—I rode my bike mile after mile, street after street, calling out to Warren.

Warren looked older than most twelve-year-olds. His frame stood taller, and the rounded sides he'd earned from eating too many homemade cookies had increased his mass. Most kids found him intimidating, and I envied him for that. Warren didn't take shit; he gave shit. People noticed him for the right reasons, not the wrong ones, like me. He acted more like Mom. He could hold his own in a fight, unlike me, but I couldn't ignore the hollow aching in my chest. He'd never done this before. The worst thoughts drove through my mind: beaten, kidnapped, hit by a bus. Not one of those things was true. If something that awful had happened, word would have gotten back by now. Someone would have told me, I reasoned with myself as I pedaled further and further into the night.

The trees grew lush, dense. Houses became fewer and fewer, and I'd not been able to read a street sign for at least seven miles. My whole life had been spent in this town, but the night changes things. The fog thickened, but I wasn't going home until I found Warren. I couldn't lose him too. It would have been wise to have stayed on the main streets. Naturally, that would have been the right thing to do, for me, but not for Warren. If he was traveling along these roads in an attempt to escape our uncomfortable home life, he would have walked down those that were less traveled. I kept calling out his name, watching for familiar signs and trying to figure out how I'd gotten so lost in my effort to find my lost brother.

I knew I was far off from town, as all I began to see was farmland—corn stalks and dark emerald green fields encased by mud-brown fences. I'd counted only two street lights for the last five miles, when I saw a dim flicker of light shifting through the trees. It looked bright and orange, like there might be some idiot kid camped out in the clearing with a fire and a sleeping bag in hopes of living in the woods for the rest of his life. I veered off the road, letting my bike fall to the ground, and stalked out into the tall woods. Warren would hear it for this one. There wasn't any reason for me to take the heat for him. I followed the glowing light, still shouting Warren's name. And my voice caught, as I heard a slight humming, an almost buzzing coming out through the brushes.

Warren wasn't in the clearing. I had made my way deeper into the trees, too far off for me to see my silver bike, when I saw what the shimmering light had been. It was difficult for me to process the lone glowing orb of pure light floating in front of my eyes. But it wasn't an illusion. Magic danced before me. I knew I wasn't dreaming, but I also knew this light couldn't be real. Hallucinations weren't common in people my age, but with the fog, and the strain in my eyes from the night ride, I knew I couldn't trust what I was seeing. But for whatever reason—if you asked, I surely couldn't tell you—I followed the little light.

A small pond engraved water into the empty field. The light led me there. It skimmed across the water, and I kneeled down expecting to see a blurrier version of my features. But as I looked upon the water I saw her there. Her honey-colored eyes shined out through the mist, and I couldn't wonder why, because I was seeing her face again. I saw the faint frown lines around the corners of her down-turned mouth. My mom's face reflected off the water's surface. Her dark brown hair rippled in the water, and I could even make out her olive-toned skin in the dim light of the moon.

Surely, I was losing my mind. My mom was dead. I'd been there the day they buried her, listening to the unfriendly, small-town whispers about my father's absence. I didn't care about my sanity, though, because I knew I was seeing her, or at least my mind's recollection of the way she looked. My hand reached out toward the water to touch her. I said nothing, but as I grazed the water's surface, the faded image of my mom disappeared.

The tiny light returned to bounce around in my peripheral vision. I glanced up at it. The light moved closer toward me, blinding me, and then I felt something jump down my throat. My mind ached. My insides burned, and the light disappeared. I fell back onto the ground, stared up at the brightening sky, and closed my eyes.

The morning mist rolled in through the plains as I woke. It was morning, but the day's color was still muted and dull. I couldn't have been disoriented for more than an hour, but my neck had stiffened. It was a failed night, and I needed to get home. Warren's disappearance would be a bigger job than some kid with a limp could handle. My bike was long gone, I decided, after about 45 minutes of searching for the way I'd entered the clearing. I was afraid to get even more lost, so I gave up on finding one of my few possessions and followed the sounds of cars passing on the freeway. My plan was to follow the road until I found a gas station with a payphone that I could use to call Liza. I knew my uncle would be passed out in the hall bathroom in a pool of his own vomit. I walked along the freeway with caution. Middle-aged moms told tales of children who died on the freeway thinking that all drivers would stop for them. But I knew better. The world was full of crazy, selfish bastards.

I'd only gone a few feet when I glanced behind me at the sound of a truck horn. It was a dark blue, newish Chevy Silverado. The car belonged to Elliot. Rumors about Elliot Way being the prettiest girl in Lake Odessa reached as far as East Lansing. She lived on my block and was a senior at the high school I'd be going to next year. Her dad owned a beauty supply store near downtown, and her mom taught gymnastics at the YMCA. And Elliot, well, she was beautiful. She would babysit me and Warren when my parents went out for dinner and a movie. I used to spy on her while she sat in our living room thinking that I was in my room sleeping. I'd watch her watch television and talk on the phone about nothing for hours on end. She never did anything interesting, but I liked staring at her perfect face. She had the biggest blue eyes I'd ever seen. Her figure was telling, but she often wore baggy jeans with loose fitted cut-off tops that made the lines of her frame more difficult to decipher.

There were other pretty girls in Lake Odessa. But there was something about Elliot that drew everybody in. She was striking, and when she smiled it made you feel like she was warming herself only to you, to make you feel better.

Elliot pulled the Silverado over to the side of the road and opened the door. I hobbled toward the car, jumped in, and slammed the door. Normally, I would have been embarrassed to have someone see me rush like that, teetering and tottering from one leg to the other, but I was desperate to get off the freeway. Not only had I obsessed about Elliot ever since she used to babysit me and Warren, but now she'd personally saved me from being mauled by traffic. Her long, wavy blonde hair framed the sharp angles of her face. She smiled at me, and I had to look away. It was too much—almost like staring into the sun.

"Stephen," Elliot squealed and pulled me in to a loose embrace, making sure our chests didn't touch. I felt a sting of disappointment as I glanced down, noticing she wasn't wearing a bra and that the cool morning breeze was having an effect on her. I shifted in the car seat and turned toward the window, trying to play it cool. Playing it cool with Elliot was a lost cause, though. She had seen me running around my house in Spider-Man pajamas. She would never think of me as cool after having witnessed that.

"What are you doing out here, sweetie?" she asked me quietly as she popped her gum. Her voice was barely audible as some teenaged pop star crooned "sugars, daddies, and I-love-yous" in a high-pitched screech, blaring from the satellite radio. I never listened to music, so whoever was singing was foreign to me.

"Warren's missing," I said. "He didn't come home last night. I've been up and down these streets all night looking for him. I can't believe this shit. He's never done anything this stupid before."

"How could Warren be missing?" She asked like she didn't want me to really respond. "I saw him standing out at the bus stop this morning." Her tone was matter-of-fact, almost pacifying. It was the sign of things to come. Maybe after last night everyone was going to start treating me like a schizophrenic? My mind had outrun me. I missed my mom, more than I realized. Feeling feelings had never been easy for me, and I hadn't given myself time to grieve. That's all that light thing was—me losing my goddamn marbles. I'd need to collect them at some point, but for right now all I could do was try to forget. I still felt numb, though, and a bit hollow. I buried the feeling.

"Did you forget that I was here?" Elliot asked, running her grip along the steering wheel. Her eyes focused on the road. She didn't even turn to look at me. "Where am I taking you, Stephen?" She paused and faced me. "School or your house?" She knew about my uncle. The whole town knew, but they did nothing to protect me, to save me. And I didn't give a shit. I'd save myself. Besides, it would probably have just made things worse if anyone else tried to get involved. I knew the cops wouldn't do anything. Uncle Kasey was a bastard from hell. Nothing could change him.

"School." My words came out clipped. The vibes between us turned chilling, and I ignored it. I couldn't go home, and she knew why. School had already started anyway. If Elliot cared she'd say something, and she didn't. We drove toward the school in silence, with the exception of Elliot's gum popping. It was something I knew she'd outgrow, but it almost made her unattractive. An hour passed before I saw something I recognized—Mr. Patterson's cluttered yard with his dried out maple trees.

Mr. Patterson worked as the school guidance counselor. He lived on the outskirts of town, and his house wasn't a sight I was familiar with, but I'd seen it a few times when my mom used to drive us into Lansing. No one drove us into Lansing anymore.

It was 10:07 AM on a Tuesday, and all the early morning rushing had ended. I had eight minutes before the next bell, and without my books I should be able to make it to English on time. Trish and Liza were probably worried.

"Thanks for the ride," I said to Elliot, sounding more like a frustrated adolescent than I ever had. Why did I expect her to care about me? She was as vapid and self-absorbed as they came. Her beautiful face didn't equal a caring person.

"Bye, Stephen—talk to you later. I'm sorry about your mom," she said, still smacking her gum. She asked, but the way she asked irritated me even more, "Any word from your dad?"

I shook my head and walked toward the front office. Mrs. Smith, a short and frail middle-aged woman with bright red nails sat at the front desk, talking on her cell phone. She held the phone to her shoulder and stood up once I approached.

"I'm surprised to see you strolling in at this time, Stephen," Mrs. Smith said. "I don't think I've ever seen you come in late to school. Something wrong?" she asked.

"Just overslept," I exhaled. In my mind, that was a dead giveaway that I was lying.

"Well, here's your tardy slip," she frowned at me. "No more oversleeping."

I raced to my locker—71 steps—then dashed down the hall to Ms. Wright's English class. Someone bumped into me, knocking me off balance as I made my way through a crowd of faceless adolescents. I turned my head back to see Jared standing there. I glared at him knowing he'd been the one to bump into me, and he walked toward me.

"Something wrong, hop-along?" Jared said, boring his

eyes into mine. He'd bumped into me on purpose. Jared was looking for a fight, and I didn't want to give him a reason to embarrass me. Everyone in the hall watched us, waiting for me to say something. I shook my head at him and looked down at my books.

"That's what I fucking thought, loser," Jared said and turned his back on me. I pictured myself kicking him in the back of the head, but thought better of it and headed to class.

When I walked into my English class, everyone was already seated, but they were jabbering, so I knew Ms. Wright hadn't started teaching yet. The seat between Trish and Liza was empty because they always saved it for me. They turned to me when I walked in and sat down. Both staring, not speaking. Liza was first.

"What happened to you? You look like you slept in a cornfield," she guffawed and looked at Trish for a confirmation of this hilarious observation.

"No shit, Sherlock," I snapped. "Was Warren at the bus stop this morning?"

"Yeah, why wouldn't he be," Trish said, absentmindedly running her hands through her smoothed-out curls. I stared at her dark skin as it glinted. The morning light shimmered through the classroom windows making her skin look like copper. Things between Trish and I had gotten weird since school started. I'd known Trish almost as long as I'd known Liza, but our friendship was different. Liza treated me like an annoying little brother, but Trish, she treated me like I meant something to her. She always boosted me up, helped me, even when I didn't ask for any help, and she really understood me. Trish understood me more than Liza, more than my mom.

Most people didn't get me. The kids at school found me strange, arrogant, and off-putting. I liked taking control, especially when the teacher assigned group projects. The other kids weren't as smart, and I was usually right about most things, but they didn't like that. It made kids like Jared the Terror want to punch my face in, but I was good at staying hidden when I needed to.

I tried blending in with the others, but I was a weird kid, unlike most. The limp was one thing, but I did a lot of shit to myself. I read, like all the damn time, even during lunch. I kept big bulky sci-fi books with me wherever I went. The other kids were all into reality television, while the only two shows I ever watched were Trigun and Full Metal Alchemist—both dark, animated Japanese cartoons. My interests varied, and I preferred it that way. I wanted to figure out what I liked and didn't like on my own, and I hated when other people tried to decide for me. That was something my mom used to do. If I wanted to buy one pair of sneakers, she'd spend the next two hours in the shoe department at Meijer trying to convince me that I wanted a different pair. Trish acted that way too, but I didn't mind it most of the time. She thought she knew better than most, better than me. And I liked that about her.

But what had made things so awkward between me and Trish was me. Before this summer, I hadn't ever really looked at Trish. Now I had, and I couldn't reverse what I'd seen that first day back at school. She walked down the hall that day with a beacon of light surrounding her, and I could have sworn I heard a harp playing in the distance.

Everyone noticed the change, not just me. Trish was growing up, beautifully, and I kept my distance. I couldn't be myself around her anymore. I blanked out whenever I stared at her for too long. And I often stared at Trish for too long, which made her nervous around me.

The cycle hadn't broken. And if I kept up this weirdness, she might get fed up and write me off for good. A part of me worried that once high school started, she'd abandon me and Liza for the cool kids. She wasn't the goofy, dark-skinned girl with glasses and big beads in her braids anymore. Her dad had landed some big executive job a few months ago, and the money had made a difference for Trish's mom. Her mom used to get all of her clothes from the Salvation Army. Now, they came from the malls out in Holt County. Trish was changing. She just didn't know it yet.

"Did something happen with your uncle again?" Liza asked.

Trish rolled her eyes at me and turned around to face the front of the class. Damn, she had asked me a question and I just sat there staring, overthinking every detail and missing the big picture. As smart as I was, it would be my lack of social skills to kill me off.

"Stephen," Liza raised her voice.

"Nothing happened. Warren didn't come home last night. I went out looking for him…"

"And what?" Trish turned around again.

Ms. Wright silenced the class, and I didn't get to answer Trish. Not that I would have answered her. She already thought I was crazy; no need to add "delusional" to that list of flaws.

# CHAPTER 3

# SOME KIND OF BULLY

S TUDENTS RUSHED DOWN crowded halls, heading toward lockers or classes, making their way to the places they belonged. It was lunchtime at Pinewoods Middle School. But all that mattered to me was finding Warren. He was going to tell me where the hell he was last night, and why I'd been forced to search for him. Warren and Sam devoured their lunch out by the bleachers. Kids ate in the school courtyard because the cafeteria was overcrowded. Once the cold set in, eating outside was no longer an option, so many were trying to make the most of the autumn weather. And by autumn weather, I mean the temperature was still in the mid-thirties. This was Michigan, where kids wore shorts just because it wasn't snowing yet.

My next class was Science, again with Trish and Liza. We had lunch right after it. Eighth grade was divided into three teams: A-Team, B-Team, and C-Team. Trish, Liza, and I were on C-Team, which was for the smart kids. B-Team was for the mediocre, and A-Team was for the downright dimwitted. We all knew this was how our grade was set up, but for whatever reason the teachers and administrators tried to mask it.

Trish asked me where I was going as we walked out the classroom doorway. I hurried down the hall and shouted to her that I was off to find Warren.

As I made my way into the courtyard, I heard a few giggles at my wobble of a walk that normally I would have ignored. I felt different today, though. I couldn't place it; there was a strength within me, a sudden internal pull that I knew I shouldn't reject. And so, instead of letting this pair of chatty sixth-graders lay complacent in their mocking, I stopped short.

"Are you laughing at me?" I asked with conviction. They stared. I moved closer. "Did you just hear what I asked you?" The two little girls stared up at me with guilt pouring out of their eyes. "You shouldn't laugh at people who're different than you," I told them. "It will only make it harder to not laugh at yourself for your own bit of difference." Their faces turned blank. "I mean, there's something about you that's different, right? If you accept me, then it will be easier to accept yourself for being different." They still didn't catch my meaning, and they turned and walked away from me, back toward the school.

I looked up at the bleachers, and Warren wasn't there. Neither was Sam the Man. A crowd of students chanted and jeered near the basketball court. They all huddled together, watching something I couldn't see. I made my way over, slowly this time to avoid giggles. My arms broke through the crowd. With enough pushing and nudging I was able to see what was causing all the chaos. Warren was there, in the center of the crowd, bobbing and weaving, balancing back and forth from one foot to the other in a way I'd never seen before. His face was all scrunched up, angry—he had made a habit of looking that way lately. He glanced at me like he didn't recognize me, or he didn't care that I was there. I watched his eyes dart to the opposite side of the crowd, and standing there in almost the same boxer's stance as Warren was Jared the Terror.

Jared was the most hated kid in school. Maybe even the most hated kid in town. His presence was like a bulldozer, mulling down the halls and destroying anything in its path. Jared didn't care who he hurt, as long as someone suffered. He was a loose cannon; there wasn't anyone who could control him. I wasn't even sure how old he was. He was in my grade, although I was certain he should have been in high school by now. Jared was the reason I never rode the bus in the morning.

He had no remorse, not even for himself. He lived with his dad. I'd heard that his mom had run off to be with some other man, and I didn't blame her, although the town did. Jared's dad worked at the same factory as Uncle Kasey. It was one of the few factories left in the Mitten since Flint had shut down almost completely. Jared was the kind of guy that as soon as you saw him coming, you turned and went in the opposite direction. He was on A-Team, and so we never interacted. He used to toss tangerines at the back of my head in the school cafeteria and trip me up in the halls. I never stood up to him. I let him do it.

I watched as they fought. Warren dodged a blow from Jared and struck him hard in his left side. Jared looked unaffected. Warren was big for his age, but Jared was the size of a barn yard. He took the hit, stared at Warren, and then jolted toward him. Their bodies collided and they both fell down to the ground. Jared was on top of Warren, pinning him down in a chokehold, crushing his windpipe. This was where my brilliance usually failed me. I was too much like my dad. I hated thinking about him—I hated that I was just as much of a coward as he was. He never stood and fought, he always ran, but I couldn't let this gorilla beat the shit out of Warren. I was skinny, but I was taller than the both of them. I closed my eyes tight then jumped on Jared's back and punched him as hard as I could. Quick blows landed all over his neck and head. I couldn't focus on aiming, just hitting.

"Get the fuck off me!" Warren kept shouting.

"I can't! I can't move!" Jared replied.

All the screaming silenced. There was nothing, and I felt frozen, as if my hands weighed a thousand pounds, and the punches I threw were punishing my limbs. Some-one grabbed the back of my jean jacket and pulled me off Jared and Warren. It was Coach Miller. He held us at either side of his bulky frame, his hands gripped tightly to prevent any more violence.

"What's going on?" Not a sound came from any of us. "I better get some answers in the next five seconds or I'm calling all of your folks!"

"We were just messing around," Jared said. "Me and Warren were play-fighting, slap-boxing, and this fuck-ing cripple…"

"Watch your mouth!" said Coach Miller. "There's no

fighting in school, real or not. Keep it up and you're both off the hockey team."

Coach Miller stared at Warren. "Do you even want to be on the team anymore, Warren? You haven't been to practice since your mom died."

I groaned. Coach Miller didn't know what sensitivity was.

"He'll be back," Jared answered for Warren. "Not shit else in this town besides hockey."

My eyes shot to Warren, and he nodded, staring down at his sneakers to avoid the questions in my eyes.

"So no more staged fights in the schoolyard?" Coach Miller asked, and Jared and Warren nodded at him. "Are you alright, Stephen?"

I shook my head. "I thought they were serious," I said. "I was just trying to help Warren."

Warren laughed. But it wasn't Warren's laugh; it was someone else's. The laugh was vindictive, coaxing. It belonged to Jared. And Warren had acquired it. I tried to block it out.

"You can't even walk," Warren said to me. "What makes you think I'd need you to help me fight?" He laughed again, shaking his head, not looking at me.

"Get to class, all of you!" Coach Miller said. He walked off back toward the gym, leaving me to face Warren and his new best bud, the biggest asshole in school. Jared patted Warren on the shoulder, pulling him back toward the school, and away from me. He started to walk off, and I started to let him. But I was pissed.

"Where the hell were you last night?" I called to him.

"None of your damn business," he muttered. His back

turned away from me. I hobbled in front of him, forcing him to look at me.

"I was out looking for you all night. Don't pull that shit again," I said.

"What the hell are you going to do about it? You can't do shit, Stephen. Except for tell Uncle Kasey, and in case you haven't noticed, he doesn't care about either of us. He'll just pound your face in for even talking to him."

I stood there still, blocking his and Jared's passage into the school. There was nothing I could say. I could only stand there breathing heavily, knowing I was powerless. He didn't have to listen to me, but I hoped he would.

"You may not care about yourself, asshole, but I still do. You better be home after school." He laughed again and crossed his arms across his chest. "I'm not playing with you."

"I'll be home when I want. Get out of my way."

My brain stormed as I watched his hands move toward me. He pushed me back, hard, and I toppled over onto the ground like a toddler, nothing like the big brother I needed to be. I watched them from the ground as they walked away from me. There wasn't anything I could do. No matter what I said, Warren was too bitter to hear a word of it. He had that chip on his shoulder that you always hear old people talk about. It was up to him whether he would keep it.

A few minutes later, I sat at a lunch table in the school cafeteria feeling unreasonably sorry for myself, and mercilessly taking out my frustrations on Trish and Liza.

"Are you going to talk about it at all?" Liza breathed, a sigh in her voice as she anticipated the outcome.

"Nope," I said and popped a French fry in my mouth.

"Warren's off his rocker, hanging out with that demon-child Jared, and you're just going to let him. What if he...?"

"What if he what, Liza? What if he hurts himself or someone else? There's nothing I can do. He's clung to that ape of a kid, and if that's what he wants, why should I care?"

"Well, you know what this is all about, don't you?" Trish finally spoke. She'd been avoiding eye contact with me since I sat down. I waited. "After your mom died," she almost mouthed the words, her voice was so quiet, "you were different, Stephen. We couldn't get you to talk to any of us, about how you felt, and you still haven't really, but you had us there to force you. No one's forcing Warren to talk about it, so he's keeping it all bottled up. He needs more friends who are girls. You can't talk to guys about your feelings."

"He could talk to me," I said.

"Why would he bother, when you haven't talked about it? He probably thinks no one cares about how he feels," Liza said as she picked at the egg in her salad. "He's turned icy. I'm just surprised you're not worried, Stephen."

"I'm not worried about Warren," I lied. "He'll come around when he's ready."

They both rolled their eyes at me. And I didn't care. I wasn't going to open up to them about how worried I really was. This was something different. I couldn't talk about it. I needed time. Just like I needed time before I was ready to talk about everything I was dealing with. It was becoming a bit much, though. I felt weak, restless. They wouldn't understand.

Coleman, a short, blond-haired boy in our homeroom walked over to our lunch table.

"I brought you something, Liza," he said, watching us all with careful eyes.

Coleman was the gross, smelly kid in our class who obsessed over Liza. He embarrassed her most of the time. So I wasn't surprised when Liza ignored him, but Trish turned his way.

"That's sweet of you, Coleman," Trish said. "What did you bring?"

Coleman reached inside his pocket and pulled out something that looked like paper, but the color was light brown. I noticed a bug-like abdomen and had to stop myself from laughing when I realized what he'd brought Liza.

"They're Katydids," Coleman said. "Well, not anymore; this is the skin they shed." He held it out for us to see, and Liza gagged. Coleman didn't notice. "They remind me of you, Liza, and I want you to have them."

"That's disgusting. Leave me alone," Liza groaned, and she stared at Coleman until he walked off. "He's so weird," she said. "The next time he comes over here no one's allowed to talk to him. Do you hear me, Patricia Adams?"

Trish ignored her and changed the subject. "Want to ride bikes home after school?"

"Can't," Liza said. "I've got piano lessons. My mom's picking me up after school."

"I thought you gave up on the piano," Trish asked Liza.

"I wanted to. I mean, I don't think it's for me. But I'm

no quitter. And the teacher thinks I'm awful, so I'm going to prove that old crow wrong."

Trish giggled. Her eyes lit up, and I could see how much she admired Liza's tenacity. It really was one of her best qualities. Liza leaned across the lunch table and ruffled my dark-blond hair so that it fell in front of my eyes. "But Stephen will go, won't you?"

I moved the hair from my face and turned to Trish. "I'll walk while you ride, but my bike's incognito until I can afford to buy a new one."

"What happened to your bike?" Trish asked.

I shrugged. "Lost it when I was out looking for Warren."

It was the truth, but still it felt like a lie.

"You loved that bike. Do you want us to help you find it? You won't be able to afford a new one," Trish said.

"I know that," I snapped. I didn't need her reminding me of how helpless I'd become since my parents had abandoned me. "It's gone for good. I'll just have to sell something to replace it. There's no way I'm riding the bus in the morning."

"Warren takes the bus," Liza said. And I said nothing. I didn't give a crap about Warren. No one said anything else after that, and we sat in silence. My grumpiness ruined people's days.

"Stephen," Trish pleaded. "Will you stop? You're making it hard to make excuses for you. You need to start being nicer to us. I get you're going through a tough time, but we're only trying to help you. We're not trying to be mean, but anything we say rubs you the wrong way."

It sounded like she was talking about Warren, not me.

I couldn't lose my only two friends. I'd have to get better at hiding what I was thinking.

"I'm sorry," I muttered. "I'll watch it."

"Well, let's do movie night at my place Thursday," Trish said, switching subjects. "My dad just bought a huge flat-screen, and guess what?" She beamed. "It's a 3-D TV! It freaking rules. You guys are going to love it." Liza and I were silent. Trish was changing; she just didn't know it yet.

The lunch bell rang, and the rest of the day passed without any more drama. Warren avoided me, and I was glad. I didn't even want to look at him, and as far as protecting him from Uncle Kasey—he could forget about it. I wasn't going to be the buffer anymore. I'd let him take his licks; maybe it would help him to appreciate me more. The weight of living had become heavier with each step. Worrying about Warren was something I'd have to shake.

When classes ended, I walked to Trish's locker to wait for her. I was nervous to see her. This was the first time we'd been alone since I'd started acting like there was no hope left for humanity. I was still wearing the same clothes I had on yesterday, but no one had said anything. I didn't have my backpack, so I'd grabbed a sci-fi book from my locker to stash my homework inside. Trish strolled toward me, books pushed tightly against her chest. She smiled, white teeth on dark skin, absolutely beautiful. I couldn't take my eyes off her. My awkwardness forced me to look down. It was the fullest feeling I'd ever experienced when she stared back at me like that, a longing in her eyes. I wished I knew what she was thinking.

"You ready?" she asked me. Her eyes shifted from side to side. I nodded and watched her take a few things out of her locker and stow them away in her large knapsack. She was wearing this dark gray sweater, which was long enough to have been a dress. Her thick, jet black hair was done in big curls that fell to her shoulders.

"Stop staring at me," she whispered.

"I wasn't," I said.

"You were."

"Sorry, you just... you look different, Trish. I can't help it."

"My mom bought this dress," she said, touching a bit of the fabric. "Now that my dad has this job, she doesn't worry about the stuff she used to. She likes buying me stuff. I never even have to ask anymore."

"And your dad doesn't mind her spending so much?"

"If he does, he hasn't said anything. Ever since he took this job in Detroit, he's gone all the time. We never see him. When he is home, it's like he's not there. Like a zombie or something. Always checking his phone, click-clacking away at his laptop."

"Do you miss him?" I asked as we walked out the entrance to the school. We walked along a trail past the courtyard littered with trees.

"I didn't know what you meant at first," she admitted as we walked a fair distance apart from one another. "But yeah, I do miss him. I feel bad though. I mean, it's not like... it's not like what happened with your mom, so I don't want to be selfish about it," she said, not looking at me. "Why won't you talk about her?"

"It's not that I don't want to," I said. "I just don't know if I can." She looked confused. "Think of it this way," I said and immediately switched into animated mode, using my hands as paddles to fuel the conversation. "There's this wave of water rushing in, and if it hits it's going to destroy a whole city, everything that's been built, right?" Trish nodded. "So, you build a dam to protect the city, to protect yourself from that wave of emotions."

"That doesn't sound like the right thing to do," she whispered.

I shrugged. "It might not be the right thing to do, but for right now, it's the only thing that can be done. I haven't forgotten her. I just know I can't deal with her loss yet. I'm not ready. I need to be in a better place."

"I don't think you get to choose," Trish said, looking straight at me.

## CHAPTER 4

# HOME IS WHERE THE BODY ACHES

TRISH AND I didn't say much else on the walk home. She left her bike at school, saying that she would just take it home the next day. We parted ways at her driveway, as my house was a few more blocks down. She walked off from me, and I stood there at her drive, watching, as she shut the front door. But then she waved at me from her living room window. I was surprised she didn't invite me inside, but then again I wasn't. Maybe she was feeling a bit of the same intensity that I was. I hoped for it, even though I had no clue if it was true.

It was cold, but the sun was bright as the seasons changed. I walked around town for a bit, a little afraid to go home and face Uncle Kasey. I decided to make my way downtown to the ancient Five and Dime store for a pop and a bag of chips. Three older boys stood outside the store, leaning against the building, talking and throwing bits of trash at one another. I steadied myself into a seated position on the street curb. I lay my back against one of the rusted, wrought-iron street lamps, and started munching on the bag of chips.

There was an empty brown-red bench that I could have sat at instead, but I decided to leave it for someone else who might have had a more difficult time walking. I listened to the teenagers talking, and watched a few cars go by. Downtown Lake Odessa wasn't very busy on the weekdays. The compact, little city was filled with very few shops and restaurants that were all mushed together like faded stucco townhouses.

The city looked its age, maybe even older, but from where I was sitting all I could see were yellow, orange, and red trees rolling on for miles. We didn't have mountains in Lake Odessa. We had trees, magnificent trees that told stories with their branches, and the serene Lake Jordan of course. The chill in the air made me pull my jacket tighter around me. I had on black jeans and my scuffed up red Converse, "chucks" I heard Trish call them once.

"I'm telling you I saw something crazy," said the tallest boy of the three. "It was like this tiny ball of light out in the woods near the old fairgrounds. It looked like a fallen star or something." The other boys laughed.

"I'm sure you saw something, but it wasn't a star," another boy said. "It was probably just a firefly or a reflection. You sound crazy. Just how high were you?"

"Shut up, I wasn't high. I know what I saw, and it looked like a star landing on Earth," I heard the lanky boy say, and they walked inside the small, maroon-colored church at the corner. My insides burned, and my ears felt red. I thought about following the older boys inside the church, but there wasn't anything else to hear. Whatever I had seen was an illusion. Who cares if that older kid thought he might have seen it too? There was nothing to see, there was nothing to say.

I threw my trash out and headed home, feeling more abnormal than I ever had before. I ran my hands along my jeans, brushing the chip crumbs off the dark denim, when I felt the cell phone still there in my pocket. It was bulky, but I'd been so preoccupied that I'd forgotten about it. I took it out and switched it on, just to make sure it was still working. It was, and unfortunately my dad was still pathetically texting the damn thing at least three times a day. He had so many words for a dead person, and nothing to say to me or Warren. A part of me wondered if he would ever come back; the other part didn't give a damn.

No one was home when I walked into the old brown house. The yellow kitchen hummed with loneliness, but I felt something there. It felt like my mom was there with me. It was like I could see her standing there making the white bean chili that had earned her a bit of small-town fame. I saw Dad there too, wrapping his arms around her waist, surprising her from behind. The two of them laughing, loving each other. I didn't know how good I'd had it, and now I would never see that again. I leaned against the wall in the foyer and slid down to the floor, landing so that I was sitting on the heels of my feet.

The tears wouldn't come, but I felt the hole in my chest growing. My heart hardened as I fought the hurt, as I fought my despair. I didn't want to forget my mom, but I didn't want to think about her either. This wasn't something I could easily escape—staying in this house day after day, holding on to the pain of it. The pain of her calling out Warren's name and mine first thing in the morning to wake us for school. Her laughter, her smile—all those memories flitted in my mind.

The constant encouragement she had given me for all my endeavors, especially the crazy ones. She had even thought the whole nuclear physicist thing was a good idea. My dad had thought I was making it up when I told them that was what I wanted to do with my life. He laughed, envisioning me becoming a more sinister version of a mad scientist. But Mom thought it was brilliant. She thought I was brilliant.

The day of her funeral, it didn't hit me, not until now. Even as they lowered the casket, I had somehow kept my emotions in check. But now, being in this house, feeling helpless, lost and alone, I had to face the fact that she was really gone. I wouldn't ever see her again. Her time had ended, and my time with her was over. Being with my mom had made me feel like falling. I'd been careless, completely dependent upon her, knowing she would always be there to care for me. But now she wasn't. Our lives had been beautiful, perfect. And all I'd ever done was complain. I got upset when she asked me to do the dishes or to help her bring the groceries in from our light blue Volkswagen. I never thought about everything she did for us. I couldn't remember ever saying thank you.

She had worked at IGA, the only grocery store in town, at least 50 hours a week, while my dad managed the hardware store inside the downtown square. She took care of us, and I never thought about just how hard she worked inside and outside the house. There was always a smile on her face, laughter in her voice. Everything was a joke to her, even things that weren't that funny. She would always say, "I love you, Stephen, more than anything my little life could ever give," and then she'd pause, "but God loves you more."

I wasn't sure if I believed in God anymore. It was hard for me to believe in anything now. The future blurred and rippled out of my vision. It was difficult to see what would happen next, and that was something I hadn't had to think about much before. Mom would want me to keep trying, though. She'd want me to look out for Warren. And I had to do what she wanted now.

I felt like she was watching me, like she could see me struggling against mourning her. But I knew she wasn't really there. I knew she couldn't see me anymore. She wouldn't be here to see me off to college, and I wanted to make the most of her memory. I was her son, and I had to do something to make all of her faith in me worthwhile. Wherever she was, whatever happened after death, she would be proud of me. I would make my time on this Earth count—for her. She gave me this life. And that woman wanted me to be great, and not just because I was her son, but because I was different.

"Be that, Stephen," she would say to me.

"What?" I would ask in reply.

"Exactly as you are," she would laugh. "You're going to make me millions one day, my too smart boy." I could still hear her voice, calling out to me from the kitchen. She never said stuff like that to Warren. My mom cared about Warren, but she knew he would be normal. He was more sociable, daring, more outgoing than I would ever be. But he didn't stand out, and so he'd never be forced to find his own way. He would stay in this town. I would leave. My mom had always known that.

Keys jangled at the front door. My throat dropped to my stomach, but I didn't move. If Uncle Kasey saw me like this, he'd say some shit to hurt me more. But I couldn't pull myself together. I wasn't broken, but a few pieces of me were lost inside my head.

The door opened.

"You alright?" Warren asked, sounding more like himself than he had in weeks.

"No," I lied honestly. I was alright, but I wasn't alright.

He laughed, his face falling back in time to the fake fight on the blacktop. "You look like you're about to cry. Get up and fix your face before *he* gets home." Warren didn't like saying Uncle Kasey's name unless he had to. He was that disgusted with him, but there was something else there in what he'd just said. His words sounded solemn. I knew at once the laugh had been fake. He still cared about me.

"What are you doing here? Jared too busy making babies cry to hang out with you?"

"I still live here, don't I? And don't act like you know Jared."

"I know you're going to end up in deep shit if you keep hanging out with him."

"Well, it's a good thing you don't know anything, then."

"Why are you so pissed?" I asked with such nerve that it didn't sound like me. There was a cutting edge in my tone. It sounded like Mom.

"There's not a damn thing to be glad about." He walked toward his bedroom. "Pissed is all I've got," he said and slammed his door. Although he acted like a little shit, I knew Warren was in there somewhere. He just needed to learn to dream again. We both did.

Uncle Kasey liked when we all ate dinner together. Don't ask me why, because we knew he hated us. We were his burden, but at least he had somewhere to sleep. His girlfriend, whom my mom had forced me to call Aunt Betty, had kicked him out into the streets in August. She couldn't take his mood swings or drunken rages. And even though Mom was dying from cancer then, she had demanded we open our doors to him. He had stayed here ever since, and maybe it was a good thing. I wasn't quite sure, and I had no way of knowing if foster care would be worse. At least we got to stay at our school and in our town. Social Services would have uprooted us.

Warren eventually came out of his room to ask for help with his math homework. Reluctantly, I provided it. He still needed me. Even though he would never admit it. The kitchen smelled like sweet, salty meat and caramelized onions as I cooked Sloppy Joes for dinner. There were three things I could make for dinner—spaghetti, Sloppy Joes, and breakfast food. Uncle Kasey never cooked. He treated me the worst, and I was expected to make dinner. He never asked me to, except for that first night after Mom died, and since then it had become my obligation.

I cooked, and Warren sat at the kitchen table finishing his homework when Uncle Kasey stumbled in. He was late, and he already smelled like beer. There was a bar on the corner near the steel forge factory where he worked.

Most nights he drank there before heading home. I liked those nights because I usually didn't have to see him, but he had come home earlier tonight. His presence caused a burning panic in my gut and left an awful, metallic after-taste in my mouth.

But as he neared the two of us in the kitchen, he didn't say a single word. His eyes were glazed over like I'd never seen before. He tossed his lunch pail in the kitchen sink, snatched a beer from the fridge, and went straight to the TV room. We didn't have a living room, just one open room adjacent to the kitchen with a big screen TV in it. It wasn't plasma, we couldn't afford that sort of thing, but it was a big 42 inches, and I was proud of that. It went out sometimes during storms, and the top-left corner of the screen looked like a rainbow swirl of color. Warren had attached a magnet to it when he was nine, and the color had stayed ever since.

Uncle Kasey turned it to the sports station, and Warren got up from the table and sat on the couch, next to Dad's favorite chair. Uncle Kasey always sat in that chair, and it had never pissed me off until now. Even though my dad was the biggest coward I was sure I'd ever meet, he paid for this house. My dad had earned that chair, while Uncle Kasey had ownership of it because of a sad story, a quick and unexpected death. He treated our house like it was his castle, and Warren and I were his stable animals. Stable animals that could do tricks—like clean up after him and cook his dinners. Fat fuck. I hated him.

"What'd you do in school, kid?" he asked Warren as he propped his feet up on our coffee table. His belly hung over his jeans and sat on the tops of his thighs. He took another swig of beer, and the liquid drizzled down his chin.

"Nothing," Warren said. "Just some math and spelling stuff. I was messing around with one of the guys on the hockey team today, and Stephen tried to jump in. He thought we were really fighting." Warren laughed. "He's lucky me and Jared didn't kill him."

"What the hell were you thinking, short leg?" my uncle called to me from the living room. "You're practically a girl. Jumping in a fight... I'll show you how to fight."

"Yeah, Stephen won't do shit. Everybody picks on him," Warren said.

"But not you, Warren. Hockey's gonna make you tough. Stephen's a waste of space. He's a damn cripple, can't do shit." My uncle thought that was hilarious. "Gimpy!" he called me as if he'd forgotten my name. "Bring me a beer."

I thought about saying no, but that wouldn't have been brave; that would have been just plain stupid. And so I walked over to my dad's chair and handed my uncle the beer. I turned on my heels, heading toward the kitchen, and he tripped me up.

Laughing, he said to me, "It's not my fault you can't walk, stupid." He whispered the words as if he cared whether Warren heard what he was saying. But he didn't care. He just wanted me to hear his disgust. "When's dinner ready?"

He wanted me to get upset. That sweaty, balding walrus wanted me to say something smart back so he could hit me and feel better about himself. He wouldn't get any more self-satisfaction on my account.

"Just need to set the table," I said, getting up and heading toward the kitchen. I fixed our plates and saved my uncle's for last. While the frozen French fries browned in the oven, I lifted the top of his hamburger bun and spit in the meat. It wouldn't hurt him, but it would be hilarious to watch him eat it. He was weird about germs, it would have freaked him out, and the fact that he wouldn't know that I'd done it delighted me even more.

We all sat around the distressed, dark wooden table. Warren and I dug in, not saying a word—we usually ate in silence. Uncle Kasey drank his beer and stared at the TV screen. He laughed at something, loudly to himself as no one else laughed with him. My eyes followed his stubby, hairy hand as he reached for his Sloppy Joe. He lifted the sandwich to his mouth, and I almost exploded with laughter, but somehow I managed to stay quiet. He stopped before the sandwich could reach his mouth. He brought it close to his nose and smelled it.

"This shit smells rotten," he yelled. "I'm not eating this crap." He looked at me, and then I watched as he tossed his plate against the kitchen wall. The plate shattered, and the broken pieces fell to the ground. "You're a worse cook than your useless bitch of a mom. Clean this shit up."

I stared at the mess and turned my head toward him. "No," I said. "You clean it up. If you don't like it, then it's *your* problem. Not mine."

My uncle laughed, his lips grimacing. I'd given him exactly what he wanted: a reason to hit me. But logic eluded me as my anger took control, and I decided that I wasn't going to let him beat me. Not tonight, and not ever again. I was so done with his shit that he might as well have been a CD player.

My insides started to burn and bubble. I wanted to kill my uncle. I wanted to torture him the way he tortured me.

"What the fuck did you say?" my uncle said, chastising me. "I don't think I heard you, gimpy. Could you repeat that?"

"Fuck you," I said. "If you say another word about my mom…"

Warren pushed his chair back from the table in shock.

"I'll say whatever the hell I want. This is my house now. Forget your mom and your dad. They left you, remember? I'm all you've got now."

I threw up my middle finger at him. Uncle Kasey jumped up from the table and lunged at me. Without me touching it, the kitchen table lifted and crashed into my uncle, shoving him away from me. He fell back onto the linoleum floor, but before he could pull himself up, the TV shut off with a loud crack. Wind whistled into the dusk, beating into the sides of the house. The shaking started in my chest and then traveled out through my limbs. My anger blinded me. All I could see in that instance was hot, white light. But I could feel the fury brewing inside me, bubbling up to the top of my existence, ready to boil over.

The house trembled as my body did. The lights in the TV room and in the kitchen flickered, sending a humming noise throughout the house, just like the sound I'd heard in the clearing last night. Warren looked at me, horror-struck. The beer bottles that covered the coffee table exploded. I heard the glass shatter and the fizzing sound of the bronze-colored liquid as it spilled onto the floor. But this was not my breaking point. I could feel my anger building, and I knew I needed to calm down.

"What the hell's happening?" Warren asked Uncle Kasey.

"Stop it, Stephen," my uncle said, shouting. "Whatever the fuck you're doing, stop it before you hurt someone."

They both jumped up, but I stayed seated, wishing that my uncle's head would pop off the way the beer cap had exploded. The shaking wouldn't stop. I couldn't manage to gain control. I wondered if this was what a seizure felt like. I wondered if Uncle Kasey and Warren could see me shaking, or if I was the only one who could feel it. The light above the kitchen table went out with a loud pop as the glass broke and fell onto our plates. The sound brought me back, and I was seeing everything all over again. This really had just happened. I jolted to my room and slammed the door shut. My uncle didn't chase after me, like he normally would. He left me alone, out of anger and confusion over what had just happened. I heard him tell Warren to clean up the mess and to leave me alone for the night.

"Stephen should be out here cleaning too," Warren argued. "He's the one who caused all this shit to happen. If you hadn't pissed him off…"

"Shut the fuck up. Stephen didn't cause a damn thing to happen. It was just the wind, dumbass!"

## CHAPTER 5

# I DON'T BELIEVE IN MAGIC

THE NEXT MORNING Warren and I rode the bus to school. Matt, another kid in Warren's grade, brought his MP3 player to the bus stop and blasted Kid Cudi, the only music I tolerated, through the pulse of the chilling air. I ignored the other kids laughing and talking and stared down the road waiting for the bus to pull up. I stood beside Liza, not talking. She beamed at me when I approached the bus stop, and all I could offer in return was a faint half smile. There weren't sufficient words to describe just how tired I was. My eyes hadn't closed, not once throughout the night. I couldn't feel myself. I felt lost inside my head, trapped with no way out. I couldn't stop my mind from replaying the events from last night.

Warren kept his distance, but he kept giving me these looks every now and then like he was trying to see inside my brain, or he was just hoping the skin on my face might fall off. I can't say I blamed him. That morning, as I brushed my teeth, I kept staring in the mirror, half-expecting my skin to start melting right off my bones. The heat consumed me. October had only just started, but it was already winter. It was so cold out that morning, I couldn't feel my ears, my eyes were dry, but the rest of me was blazing.

I felt like fire.

Liza sat beside me on the noisy school bus. She chatted away about how amazing she'd been at piano lessons the night before. "You should have seen the look on the old crow's face when I nailed Für Elise. Aw, man. It was the sweetest feeling ever." She hit the back of the seat in front of us in excitement. "She won't be able to talk crap anymore, nope. I totally owned it!"

I could hear what she was saying, but it's like what I was hearing and thinking were on different tracks. There was a delay in my brain. My mind was like a disc on repeat; I couldn't stop replaying and replaying what had happened. My emotions had gone all haywire at dinner. I felt like I couldn't stop shaking, couldn't control what my brain was doing. I knew my uncle would bury it and pretend it hadn't happened. Warren would do the same, but what was I supposed to do? I didn't believe in magic, but what if there was something wrong with me? What if I needed to be locked up in an insane asylum? The world just wasn't going to give me any sort of breaks, for anything. I wanted to go back in time and forget about everything that had happened last night, and in the clearing. If I forgot, maybe the pain in my chest would stop.

"Stephen!" Liza called. "Are you even listening to me?"

"What? Yeah, 'totally owned it,' 'old crow'—I heard

every word," I said, staring out the bus window. Liza pouted her lips and slammed her back into the bus seat.

"I'm sick of everyone ignoring me," she huffed. And I felt bad, I had been ignoring her, but I couldn't think of what to say. All I could think of was what if I could do it again? If I'd done it once before, maybe it could happen again.

That was all my mind pondered as we rushed off to homeroom. Trish was already there. Her mom must have dropped her off that morning. Her dark hair was pulled back into a ponytail, making her eyes look even bigger. She had on a bright red sweater with light-colored jeans. Her frame was so tiny and small, almost like a miniature person. Trish hated how short and small she was, but I didn't mind it. It was just how I hated my limp. We all had those things about ourselves that we felt didn't quite match up. But Trish always made me feel better about myself, even with the limp.

"It gives you character," she told me once. "You'll be better than all of us because of it. You really should be proud. I usually forget you even have the limp. You don't draw attention to it, not like you'd expect."

I wasn't sure what she meant, but I didn't care. She said she usually forgot about the limp, and that was more than enough to skyrocket my confidence. Trish's eyes sparkled and lit up when she took me in. I wanted to smile back, but I didn't. I was still stuck inside my head, still wondering if I should try to make something happen again, or just forget the whole thing. I slid into the desk behind her and inhaled. She smelled like vanilla and roses.

It was like heaven. A tiny piece of heaven to torture me as my insides burned away.

"Stephen's being weird," Liza said, breaking me from my daze. Liza let out a small laugh at my tormented expression. "You better watch out, Trish," she said. "He keeps smelling your hair."

"I wasn't," I said, my voice raised at least two octaves higher than normal.

"Oh really, what were you doing, then?" Trish asked, turning in her chair to face me. Liza was already facing the back of the class. She sat next to Trish, her grin growing with each passing moment. Panic rushed to my face, and my head started to spin from the embarrassment.

"Something's wrong with me, you guys," I admitted in hopes they might pity me. It was going to be embarrassing to talk about what happened last night. They'd probably call me crazy, but anything was better than fessing up to Trish that I *had* been smelling her hair.

"Well, I could have told you that." Liza balled over with laughter. Trish silenced her.

"Is there something really bad going on?" Trish asked. "Is it about your uncle?"

"It's about him, but it's more about me. I've felt weird lately, like completely out of it. Something strange happened to me the night I went out looking for Warren. Then there were these older boys downtown, and last night I knocked my uncle over with the table without touching it. The house shook, and the kitchen light blew out. I've never seen anything like it, and I think I caused it."

I let out a sharp intake of breath as I blurted everything out fast enough that they couldn't understand me.

Trish and Liza glanced at each other for a second then burst into laughter.

"I'm sorry, Stephen, but that's hilarious," Trish said.

"You really think you hit your uncle with a table? Did he flip out?"

"No, I'm telling you. My mind got all sharp, all the colors in the kitchen turned vivid. It was like I was Spider-Man, but mixed with the Hulk because I couldn't control my anger. My uncle said all this nasty shit about me, my mom, my cooking, and I just exploded—literally, and the house almost exploded too."

"Well, you won't ever catch me complaining about your cooking," Liza laughed.

"No, this is serious." I needed them to understand. They had to. "I can prove it," I said. "Trish, can I see your hand mirror?" I knew she kept one. Trish had made a bad habit of checking herself out in the mirror every morning in homeroom. Liza and I used to pick at her for it, until we realized it was a lost cause.

"Yeah," Trish said, still shaking off a few fits of laughter. She reached for her jean knapsack and handed me the small, rhinestone-encrusted mirror. I grabbed the mirror, opened it, and focused my mind on breaking the glass. I'd done it before, and I could do it again. A glint of light from the window hit the pane of glass in the pocket mirror. I turned it to face them both so they could see. I envisioned the mirror cracking and shattering into tiny pieces on the classroom floor. But as we sat there, waiting for the mirror to break, nothing happened.

Not even a small cracked appeared on the surface.

I couldn't do it.

"Stephen," Trish said, reaching for the mirror. She grabbed it from me and stuffed it back in her bag. "I'm worried about you," she sighed. "I really think you should talk to the school counselor about your mom, and what's happening with your uncle. You're just a kid. You can't bear this weight alone, and you won't talk to us about it."

The bell rang for first period. I jumped up, grabbed my books, and walked out before Trish could say anything else. Talking to the school's counselor wasn't going to help anything. There was no amount of talking that could change what had happened, and what was happening. I wasn't losing it, I had absolutely lost it, and I didn't think I could go back now. There wasn't anything I could go back to.

That day, time passed like the growing of my fingernails. I couldn't face Trish or Liza. I'd made a complete ass of myself. Not a bit of it made sense to me, and I couldn't process how it had happened the night before and not today. Normally, I would have been sitting in the cafeteria at the table near the bathrooms, goofing around with Trish and Liza. But I was too busy punishing myself for my stupidity, and so I sat alone, on the bleachers, eating a dried up cheeseburger and French fries that looked like there were tiny cobwebs inside them.

My eyes fell on a chewed up No. 2 pencil sitting at the edge of the bleachers. It sat there smugly, mocking me all the while. I wanted it to move. I pictured it moving, but it wouldn't. The frustration I felt couldn't be buried. My chest rumbled as I thought about everything—how pissed I was at my dad, at my uncle, and at Warren for being so selfish. I would never see my mom again. It wasn't fair.

Life wasn't fair. Nothing on this stupid planet made any sense to me. And none of the stupid people on this planet understood me. I felt so alone. I just wanted my mom to be here, that's all. So many other kids still had their families, so why had mine been stolen from me?

Then I heard it—metal rattling on a steel bench. The pencil moved back and forth on the seat of the bleachers. And this time when I thought about it stopping, it did.

The lunch bell rang, but I didn't run back toward the school. I stayed outside for a few more minutes and practiced rolling the pencil back and forth, back and forth. It took so much energy just to get it to move—but I could see it. I was controlling it. It was the most insane thing I'd ever experienced, and while I should have been overjoyed at the fact that I hadn't completely lost it, fear started to set in.

No one could know about this.

In a small town like this, where news spread like flames through a wood, this would have to stay a secret or I'd be chased out of town. This wasn't something I could easily reveal to Trish and Liza, especially since they already believed I was crazy. I thought more about what Trish had said, though. Maybe I did need to go see the school counselor.

My insanity was evident now. I couldn't hide from myself any longer.

On my way back inside the school, my eyes caught Warren and Jared. They stood by a fountain in the entry way, teasing a sixth-grader because he carried a backpack with wheels. They had him cornered, cowering into his hands as Jared pushed him against a row of lockers. I walked toward them, my left hand holding on to the strap of my backpack, while my right curled into a fist at my side. Warren wasn't a bully. What was he playing at?

"Don't you have anything better to do?" I asked them both, holding on to my anger.

"Who the hell do you think you're talking to?" Jared said.

"I knew you were stupid. But I thought you'd be smart enough to at least understand that," I said, pacing each word with care. "Shouldn't you be trying to pass eighth grade finally? Instead of messing with little kids? We wouldn't want you failing again, for what now, the tenth time?" I knew it wasn't the tenth time, but I wanted to hurt him. Jared got pissed when people called him dumb.

Jared backed off the sixth-grader and made a move toward me. He looked like a rabid dog, but I could see the excitement twinkling in his eyes. He wanted to hurt me. The sixth-grader took his cue and raced down the hall leading out from the glass entryway.

"Mind your own damn business. Go hop along some-where else." He was in my face now, staring up at me. He was bigger, but I was still taller, just lankier—less muscle.

"I'll do whatever the hell I want," I said, willing myself motionless. I needed them both to believe that I wasn't afraid. "I'm not your flunky." My eyes shot to War-ren. He stood there still, refusing to meet my eyes. I don't think the thought to stand with me even crossed his mind, and I couldn't care. But Jared wasn't going to make me look like a coward in front of Warren. I could stand up to this asshole.

Jared and I stood there in silence, staring each other

down. He wanted me to run, but I wasn't going to. Then someone's arms flung around my neck, restraining me. The arms belonged to Warren. I saw the light pink scar on his index finger from where I'd slammed my bedroom door on his hand when we were younger. He flung our bodies against an adjacent wall of lockers and held me down while Jared punched me. I was so furious, I couldn't feel a thing—not one blow stung my skin. Jared screamed out obscenities with each punch, while Warren's arms restrained me.

My body coiled over in heat. The lights in the ceiling began to flicker. Loose-leaf paper blew through the halls. And in a second, Jared wasn't hitting me anymore. I couldn't feel his body warmth. Something had torn him off of me. His body was blown back, and he slid down the hall as if by some force beyond my understanding. The lights flickered and sparked. The metal locks on lockers rattled throughout the hall. The current within me grew stronger. The muscles around my throat tensed, and Warren loosened his grip around my neck.

"Stop it!" Warren screamed, pushing me down the hall. "Whatever you're doing, fucking stop it." He grabbed my shoulders and shook me from side to side to emphasize his point.

I closed my eyes tight, and the glass entryway shattered. "Don't fucking touch me!" I shouted. Warren jumped at the sound of the glass breaking and let go of my shoulders. I turned around to face him, but the shaking wouldn't stop. "We're not brothers," I said. "I don't know what rock you crawled out from under, but you are not my family. You're just like him," I spat. "You're exactly like your uncle. Is that what you want? You want to be fat, miserable, and drunk all the time? Stop this shit, Warren."

"What's going on?" Mrs. Williams shouted. She appeared at the top of the hall, the sixth-grader with the rolling backpack at her side. I watched her help Jared off the ground. A vacant expression clouded his eyes. I took one more look at Mrs. Williams and ran. I ran to Ms. Godfrey's Algebra class and slid into my usual seat as if nothing had happened, as if no one could get to me here.

Trish and Liza stared at me with open mouths. Ms. Godfrey pretended not to notice the fact that I'd come in late. I figured she was cutting me some slack because of my dead mom and useless dad. She continued with the math problem on the chalkboard, and one of the administrators walked in. The dark-haired man said my name, motioning for me to come with him. All the other students oohed like they'd never seen anyone get in trouble with the administrators before. But I was Stephen; I never got in trouble.

I refused to look at anyone as they escorted me out of the room, but I could hear the shock on their faces, and it caused an unfamiliar guilt to set in. They sent me, Warren, and Jared to the principal's office and gave us all two days of detention for causing general trouble. I'd never been in trouble before. I always thought it would be the worst feeling ever to have some authority figure be disappointed in me, and it was.

When I got out of detention, Trish stood outside the door waiting for me. Liza left early on Wednesdays for ballet practice. Liza's mom wanted Liza to be the best at everything. So she signed her up for piano lessons, ballet practice, and tutoring elementary school kids on the weekends. She was always busy; busy trying to prove her worth to her mom.

Trish was curious to know what had happened. I could see it there on her face, but she didn't say a word. She took one look at me and wrapped her small arms around the back of my neck, pulling herself to me. The affection surprised me. She stood up on her tip-toes to hug me, but I was too tall and her head only came up to my chest. I breathed her in once again—vanilla and roses. It was a scent I wouldn't ever forget.

We followed our usual path home, and the leaves fell, little by little as we walked along. The trees were barren for the most part, but there were still a few little golden leaves holding on for dear life. My mouth was dry, holding my tongue, and making it difficult for me to speak. Every time I looked into Trish's eyes, an endless night appeared in my mind. I listened as Trish talked a bit, about her dad's new job and how her mom seemed sadder than she ever had despite the money it brought in.

"She needs more hobbies," Trish said. "I never realized how much she relied on my dad. She doesn't have much of a life outside our family, and now that he's gone all the time, I think it's hit her, hard."

"There are plenty of hobbies she could try. Maybe the two of you could do something together," I suggested. "You know, like painting or hiking or something."

"There's not much to do around here," she said, and I nodded in agreement. "Stephen," Trish said my name like she was singing a very short song, "would you think about seeing the counselor? I think it would really help. No one expects you to handle all of this on your own."

"Worried about me?" I asked, hoping it was true.

"I am," she said, sighing without looking at me. "It's just I know you better than most people, and you've changed a lot. I mean, some of it's good. You seem more like a grown-up now, but you also seem stretched, like it's all too much. And I would really like to see you smile again. Will you go?" she asked, her voice softened.

"Well, if it means that much to you, it couldn't hurt," I said, and the smile she gave me in return warmed me all over, not like the sharp heat my anger caused, but more like the warmth of a bed on a Monday morning. I wondered if this was the feeling my dad got when he met my mom. Was this the sort of feeling that had caused Daisy Wilkes to marry a coward? I didn't check the phone again, and I wouldn't.

## CHAPTER 6

# THE TAPESTRY UNRAVELS

ELLIOT'S MOM WAS standing outside my house when I walked up to the front door. She carried several books—a few thin, some thick, tucked under her right arm. I noticed her pacing along the walkway from the drive, drumming her skinny fingers along one of the hardbacks.

"Stephen," she called out to me once she noticed I was there. "Is your uncle home?" she asked as I approached her.

"No, he won't be home for a few more hours," I told her, taking my key from the side pocket of my backpack.

She squinted her eyes trying to hide from the bright winter sunlight to look up at me. "Great, that's great. Is everything okay?" she asked. "I just wondered if Stuart has come home yet," she said as if she was asking me a question, but I knew I wasn't meant to answer. She continued, "Elliot mentioned that she found you walking out on Hwy 52 the other day. And I just thought, well Stuart must not be back, because he'd never let you do that."

"My dad's gone, Mrs. Way," I said and pushed past her to get to the front door. "He's not coming home."

"Stephen, I know you're upset about him leaving, and you have every right to be, but he will be back. Stuart wouldn't desert you and Warren."

"He already has!" I shouted, and the porch light flickered. Elliot's mom didn't notice.

"No, he hasn't," Mrs. Way said to me. "Look, I'm sorry about your dad, and I'm even sorrier about your mom, but you need to control your anger."

I nodded.

"You're not the only person who matters, and I know you get that." She paused. "I've seen how you look out for Warren. You're very mature, but you have no clue as to what your dad is feeling right now, none whatsoever, and I won't let you talk about him like that, alright?" She asked me like a mom speaking to her son, and I nodded, regaining control of my thoughts.

Elliot's mom, Bethany Way, had been good friends with my parents. She'd grown up in the house next door to my dad, and she and my mom had been inseparable all throughout high school. I only knew this because they were still very close before her death. I knew she missed my mom. The loss affected her too. Hurt shined in her eyes.

"I brought you a few things of your mom's," she said, looking down. "Here, look." She handed me the two thin books from her stack. "Here's our yearbook from junior and senior year of high school. I also brought this book of poems your mom kept with her every day when we were in school. There are a few notes of hers in there, and I just thought it would help you feel closer to her. She's never really gone, Stephen," Mrs. Way told me. "She's…"

"She's in my memories," I finished for her. "I know, Mrs. Way, trust me, I know, and thanks for these books. I really mean it." I grabbed the other book from her and started to open the front door. Her presence was comforting, but all-consuming.

"One more thing," she breathed. "And I hate to ask, but have you come across a small silver bracelet?" I stared at her, confusion written on my face. "Well, I loaned it to your mom a few years ago, and I just wondered if you would keep an eye out for it?"

"I haven't gone through any of her stuff yet," I admitted. My parents' bedroom looked exactly as it had before my mom died. Or at least I assumed as much. My uncle didn't let me or Warren inside that room anymore, not that I had any interest in visiting the ghosts that might live in there. It wouldn't be possible for my uncle to sleep there every night without that eeriness taking hold of him. But then I remembered that he hadn't slept in that room in weeks. He'd been passing out drunk, either on the couch or in the hallway outside my parents' bedroom. I decided that my mom must be haunting my uncle. It made the most logical sense to me, but I didn't believe in stuff like that.

"Well, you should. Your mom had a life before you and Warren, you know? It's a shame you don't know much about it. And I'm sure it seems scary, but it might help you feel close to her. It's good to clean out closets." Mrs. Way pulled me into an awkward hug, stared at me for a moment, and then walked off down the road toward her home.

The rest of the evening was no different than any other. Warren came home two hours later from hockey practice and went straight to his room. I made sandwiches on the Panini press for dinner, but Uncle Kasey didn't get home until late. I left Warren's outside his bedroom door, and my uncle's on the kitchen counter with a napkin over it to keep it warm. Warren wouldn't speak to me, and I couldn't look at him.

The smallest part of me had always been jealous of Warren. He didn't overthink things the way I did. Everything came easy to him. He was well-liked, popular, and he would play more hockey once he got to high school. Warren hadn't gotten stuck with a brain that was too big, or a limp in his left leg. The asshole didn't know just how good he had it. He only saw his own problems. I wondered if he even really missed Mom, or if he was just pissed about the fact that she wasn't here to take care of him anymore. It upset him that I was making his sandwiches and not her. He had probably never cared about her. I thought in spite and consumed every word.

Before bed that night, I practiced my newfound powers in the shower. I tried making a bar of soap move toward me. It took a few attempts, but eventually the bar of soap shot off the edge of the bathtub and hit me in the eye. And while I should have been upset over my injury, I was ecstatic over my progress. There was a slight aching in my chest as guilt festered there.

The world would want me to feel guilty about something like this. Especially since it seemed like anger had led me here. Rage and resentment had caused the beer bottles to break that night, and I wasn't clueless. I knew that what had gone on in the clearing the night I searched for Warren might have something to do with the changes. It was almost as if that little light had gone inside me, and it was burning away my insides and everything I had known to be true. I didn't believe in magic, until now.

My faith in myself grew. I felt stronger, more confident. I couldn't explain it, but the thought that I might be a little bit magic forced me to see myself through a new lens. It made me feel good about not being just like everyone else in this town. I'd always felt different because of the limp, but this was a much cooler sort of difference.

I didn't know what the town would think, if they would try to change me or hurt me. It had to be kept secret, but I thought it made me special. And maybe the universe knew that right then was the time that I needed to feel special—invaluable. As I lay in bed, I practiced turning the porch light off and on with my mind. Every time I heard my uncle's snoring speed up, I turned the light out just in case he woke. He'd come home around midnight and passed out in the hall again. The door to my parents' bedroom stayed locked.

When I woke the next morning, my uncle was still in the hall, slumbering and snoring outside my parents' bedroom. I stepped over his body on my way out the door. Warren was already standing at the bus stop as I walked up to it. He'd been waking up on his own as of late. Liza wasn't there. I glanced back at her house, and her mom's car was gone. Tonight was movie night, and we did this sort of thing once a week. We used to alternate houses before the accident, but now we usually hung out at either Liza's or Trish's house. Trish had already planned for it to be at her house, and if Liza wasn't there, Trish would throw a fit. So I knew Liza would be there, but I couldn't figure out why she wasn't at the bus stop.

While I stood there, waiting for the bus to arrive, I watched Elliot drive by on her way to school and saw my uncle come out of the house and leave for work. I thought about what Elliot's mom had said about going through my mom's things. Going into my parents' bedroom wasn't something I could do after school, because Uncle Kasey had claimed the room as his own when my dad hadn't come back. He didn't sleep in there, but he wouldn't let me or Warren go in there either. He'd kill me if he caught me in that bedroom, but if I went back there now while he was at work, he'd never suspect a thing. My curiosity turned to anxiousness as I thought about reliving the memories they kept in there, and I wanted to find Mrs. Way's bracelet. She'd brought me those books, and it would be a fair way to repay her, I reasoned with myself. But deep down I wondered if I'd be able to see my mom's face again, like I had in the pond that night. As time passed, it became more difficult for me to picture her face.

When the bus pulled up to the line of bundled up middle school kids, I blended in and walked up to the entrance, as if I were actually planning to get on. I wasn't, but I wanted Warren to think that I'd gotten on after him and sat up front as usual. I waited until he was getting on the bus, and then I backed away and scurried off toward our backyard. I ran through a few rows of houses, then used my key to unlock the back door. If anyone saw me they would have hauled me off to school, so I took no chances.

The books Mrs. Way had given me were hidden under my bed. I went there first and flipped through the pages, making my way to the W's, where I saw a much younger version of my mom staring back at me. Her skin looked more olive; there was less of the paleness I'd gotten so used to. Her hair fluffed out in different angles, tapered to frame her round face. She had dark brown hair, but there were lighter strands in the photo. She didn't look happy in the photo, but she didn't look sad either. Her face was indifferent, passive, and I thought about all she'd hoped for when she was my age. There was no way she could have known cancer would invade her body and kill her while she slept. Hope sparkled in her eyes—hope for her future. What a waste of hope. I studied her face, tracing its planes into my memory. She had been the best mom to me. I wasn't like other kids, neither was Warren, and that was because of her. She never babied me; she only believed in me.

I looked across the page at Mrs. Way's high school photo, and she looked just like Elliot. She had the same sharp angles in her chin, the same high cheek bones, but she had shorter blonde hair that was done up in airy curls. It looked almost like she'd stuck her hand inside of an electrical outlet. As pretty as she looked, she didn't stand out like my mom did. Something about my mom brought a light to her eyes, to her face. Bethany Way looked dim and translucent.

It took a few moments before I gathered enough courage to open the door to the room that had once belonged to my parents. I stood outside the door, willing it open with my mind, but it stayed shut. There was no way I was going in there until I could use my mind to get the door knob to turn. Getting excited or angry wouldn't work anymore, as it had before. The strong bursts of emotion that had fueled the miraculous occurrences were no longer there, and I didn't know what to do.

I backed against the opposite wall, preparing to slide down to the floor, but then I thought I heard her voice. It sounded off the walls and through the noises in the old furnace. I could hear my mom's voice carrying though our home, shouting for me to bring her a roll of toilet paper. It made me laugh. I'd almost forgotten she was human. When she got sick with cancer she became this fragile doll, this ethereal being that I felt I couldn't get close to. I always worried she would break one day, and she had. Waiting for her to die had been like a ticking time-bomb in my mind. But I still didn't get it. I never said what I wanted to say, and even though I knew I might not see her again, I didn't act that way, and now it was too late.

The sound of her voice warmed me from the inside out, and the doorknob turned. Cool air drifted in through the poorly insulated walls. The shut blinds didn't leave room for much light, and an icy blue hue colored the white walls. Our house was small, and so was their bedroom. Their queen-sized bed was pushed against the opposite wall from the closet. Sheets and pillows sprawled over the bed—no one had bothered to make it. The matching dresser sat in the left corner. I stared at the mauve, oil lamp my mom kept to remind her of her own mom. She kept an old cabinet filled with glass antique dolls. My dad only let her keep a few in the house; the others were at my grandma's. I hated those dolls. The glass eyes scared the shit out of me. The room still smelled like my parents. My dad permanently smelled like a library mixed with cheap cologne. My mom had always smelled like flour and expensive after-bath splash, which my father bought for her no matter how broke we were.

Before she got sick she always baked—pies, cookies, cakes. She was famous for her cooking and her baking. She wasn't all that proud of her job at the supermarket, but she was proud of her family and her cooking skills. She baked in excess, even when we asked her to stop. Any school event we had, she always asked, "Well, what should I bake?" The last time she asked, my reply had been, "Nothing, Mom. No one needs you to bake anything." What an asshole. Now all I wanted was for her to pour me a glass of milk and bake me her maple-pecan sticky bars while she pried for details about school that day.

I started with my dad's stuff—old ties and worn-out leather belts. There wasn't anything there that made me feel close to him. When I went through my mom's stuff, I felt different. She had a lot more stuff than my dad did. Perfumes, lipsticks, lotions, and tattered books filled with poems and short stories. I collected the books, deciding I wanted to read them. Mrs. Way's bracelet was in a box of costume jewelry. I stuffed it in my pocket and kept rummaging. My dad's golf clubs were nestled in the corner of the closet. He had boxes and boxes of unused golf balls.

An old box of photos lay on a wooden shelf. I took it down and traveled back in time throughout my parents' relationship. There were pictures of their high school prom, photos from the day I was born, images of the day they first bought this old brown house together. When I ran out of photos, I noticed a piece of cardboard at the bottom of the box. I lifted it up, and under it was a folded piece of paper. The words had been scribbled in black ink. They were faded, but I could still read them:

*Stuart,*

*You are the only man that I have ever loved. You are the only man that I've ever allowed myself to love. I've always been shut up, like a chest with an iron lock, and you found a way to open me. There's no excuse for what I'm about to say, but you know what happened, you know what he did, and I can't face myself anymore. The pain of it all eats away at everything that I've ever known—my family, my childhood. The voices, they wouldn't stop, and I just thought that if I could feel something, then maybe I could sleep again.*

*I love our life, I love our children, but most of all I love you. I love you more than anyone has ever loved another person. But I slept with another man. It hurts to write those words, so I can only imagine how you feel reading them. Hate me, please hate me for what I've done. Hate me because I can't go on anymore only hating myself. You don't know him, and you never will. He was a means to an end, and he meant nothing to me.*

*And so I am the one to destroy our marriage. When we were growing up, I always thought it would be you. I always knew that some prettier girl would come along in an attempt to steal you, and you'd be lured in like a moth by a spider, but that never happened. It was me, and I don't know if I can live with myself. Please know that I never meant for this to happen. I never meant to hurt you, and if you leave, I will understand. But know this, that even if you decide to go and never speak to me again, I will never stop loving you. There's not a thing I can do to make the way I feel about you go away. I'm a stupid woman, who betrayed the man she loves, the only person who ever cared truly for her. And I hate myself for it. I always will.*

*Your wretched wife,*

*Daisy*

CHAPTER 7

# THINGS TO SEE

MY BREATH WOULDN'T catch as my eyes lingered on those handwritten words. She'd hurt him, crushed my dad while she was still living. As if her death hadn't severed him in two. I couldn't process this, not now. This was a thing to be buried. I put the letter back where I found it and placed the box back on the shelf. The version of my mom that I'd been clinging to was ruined. She'd done this. She'd betrayed our family, and now she was gone. I couldn't ask her why or scream at her for hurting us. How could she have done this? I tried to think back. I tried to remember the way she'd been before she got sick, but I couldn't. A different Stephen had existed back then, a more selfish one, and I hadn't paid her or my father any attention. I mean, I'd known they were there, but I had thought of them as only being there for me, as if their lives existed to take care of me and not to live for themselves.

The day turned cloudy as the ugliness of winter settled

in. I sat there, in my parents' closet, and cried like a four-year-old girl who had just dropped her ice cream cone. Once it started, it wouldn't stop. The dam had been lifted, and I cried for myself and for my dad for the first time. I cried for Warren, and I even cried for my mom. She had hated herself, and I had never known. And I would never find out why or what had happened. I didn't think I would ever see my dad again, and if I did, this wasn't something you brought up. This was something you repressed. And my dad... he was still in love, still obsessed with this woman who'd done him so wrong. It didn't make sense.

I sat on the edge of my parents' bed, wanting the four walls of their room to be my sanctuary again. When I was little and a storm would come, I would hide under their bed. For whatever reason, I had felt safe here, like their presence would protect me, even when they weren't home. I wanted to feel that way again, but I couldn't. So I just sat there thinking, trying to work everything out while the day passed. I heard kids getting off the school bus, but Warren didn't walk through the door. I waited to hear him, but the sound never came. I wanted someone to save me from my thoughts.

And then there was a faint knock at the front door.

When I opened it, I saw Trish and Liza poised on the doorstep. Small raindrops fell to the ground, darkening the pavement. Liza stood several inches taller than Trish. Liza was pale with dark blonde hair, not unlike my own. She struggled with acne, and I guessed she would throughout high school. Her appearance didn't grab your attention the way Trish's face did. She looked a lot like my sister, a lot like everyone else. Trish's dark skin was like lacquer, smooth and perfect. They both looked content standing there as gentle rain clung to the lashes of their eyes. They looked just fine until they registered my expression. Their faces turned solemn, questioning. "Why did you stay home today?" Trish was the first to speak as I stared at them. "Is everything alright?"

Liza gasped as she inspected the bruise on my right eye. The soap from the night before had left a lavender-colored welt underneath my eye. "Is your uncle hitting you?" Liza asked. "Did he leave that mark?"

I rubbed at my face as if the touch would make the discoloration disappear.

"No, it wasn't him," I said. "I fell in the shower." I sounded like one of those videos about signs of child abuse they made us watch in school. They both knew I was lying. "Okay, I didn't fall in the shower, but my uncle didn't do this. I did it myself. I'll tell you about it later." I brushed off their questions and opened the door to let them inside.

"Well, why weren't you in school?" Trish asked again as she sat down on our dark red couch in the TV room. I handed her and Liza pops from the fridge.

"I'm not sure. I mean I didn't plan on skipping until this morning," I thought out loud. "Elliot's mom came by here yesterday with some old books that belonged to my mom. It just made me think that I should go through her stuff. But I could only do it while my uncle was at work, so this morning seemed like the perfect time." I shrugged.

"Seeing Elliot's mom with some old books made you want to snoop in your parents' room?" Liza asked. "Was there anything good in there?"

I thought about the letter, but I couldn't tell them.

"Not really, but it just opened up a can of worms, I guess. I wanted to feel closer to my mom, and now I just don't." I didn't know how to talk about this. I tried again, "It's like my parents had lives before me, and yeah I already knew that, but going through their stuff made it more real. And my dad…"

"You have heard from him, then?" Trish asked. She saw it on my face.

"Not directly," I said, confusing myself. "I found this." I pulled the cell phone out of my pocket—I'd been subconsciously keeping it with me since the day I found it. "He keeps sending all these pathetic texts about how much he misses her and loves her. It's pitiful. I had to stop reading them."

"Let me see," Liza said, snatching the phone from my hand. She pulled it toward her and Trish's faces. "These messages are so sad," she said.

"They're beautiful," Trish said, "beautifully sad. And he's been sending these all this time and you haven't responded?"

"Why would I respond? So he'd think I was my mom speaking to him from the beyond?"

"Just to make him feel better," Trish said. "To comfort him. You can put up that front all you want, Stephen, but we know you want your dad to come home."

"You might be right," I said, shocking them both. "Maybe I do want him to come home," I pondered. "I honestly don't know anything anymore."

We finished our drinks, and they both told me a bit about what had gone on in school that day. Warren and

Jared were fast-turning into the school's tyrants. Liza explained that they expected everyone to do anything they said no matter how crazy. She said that Warren and Jared bum-rushed a group of seventh-graders and stole their shoes. They threw them up in the big pine trees just past the courtyard.

"I don't understand why they do stuff like that. Could anyone get their shoes down?" I asked.

"No, and everyone was too afraid to tell a teacher," Trish said. "They're terrorizing everyone in their path. They need to feel powerful. And what better way than to exert some control over other little kids."

"Warren's turned into an asshole," Liza said. "He was always an arrogant jerk, but now he thinks he runs stuff. You need to knock some sense back into him," she told me.

"Only Warren can decide if he wants to change," I said. "If he thinks treating other kids like crap is going to help him in life, then let's see how it pans out for him."

"He's been skipping school with Jared after lunch," Liza said, avoiding making eye contact with me. "I don't know if it's true, but Ashley told me they go out near those abandoned warehouses to smoke pot."

My pulse quickened. I knew something big was going on with Warren, but I had to believe he wouldn't do something so stupid. Panic coursed through me, but I masked it from my two best friends. We decided to head to Trish's house for movie night, and I didn't want the two of them sitting on our couch when my uncle walked through the door. I didn't wait for Warren to come home, because he could take care of himself now. I didn't believe that, but he did, and I wanted him to see what dealing with everything on his own felt like.

The big screen was just as enormous as Trish had said. It stood out in her small home. Their family room wasn't much bigger than our TV room, and it didn't fit well. The TV looked like an eye sore, taking up too much necessary space. The room felt cluttered and even smaller than it had before. We all piled in to the space, and neither Liza or I commented on the size of the TV. Trish and Liza sat on the couch, and I sat on the floor in the space between them. Trish's mom ordered us pizza and left us to go pick up more movies and snacks. We offered to go with her, but she said it was fine. She looked a lot more glamorous since I'd seen her last, but more depressed. Traces of her tears stained the makeup on her face. Staring at her was like watching a car accident, and I couldn't look away even when Trish elbowed me.

We decided to watch E.T. and Walt Disney's Fantasia. I didn't mind E.T., it was one of my favorites, but Fantasia always put me to sleep. "It's about the music," Liza argued with me. "The music and the colors and the stories. You're just too dim to see its appeal."

"Whatever," I said. I was done arguing my point. They were both ganging up on me as they often did. Liza played the piano, and Trish played the violin in school, so they both believed music played this big role in life and beauty. I'd never thought to play an instrument, and it wasn't exactly the cool thing to do. I didn't need any more weight tipping the scale of coolness in the opposite direction.

Being there with the two of them, it helped me to forget. This was my time machine—sitting here with my two best friends watching nerd movies. We had done this before I became the most pitiful kid in town. But there was no way I was going to pity myself now. I'd discovered the gift, and I knew things would work out somehow. I wasn't sure how, or what I needed to do, but I could already feel the path changing. It could have been the changing of seasons, but I knew the change was much bigger than that— this was something tangible. I needed it to be.

"Did going through your mom's stuff destroy the town?" Trish asked.

"No, it didn't," I said. "There was some minor water damage, but the town is still intact." I turned around and smiled up at Trish. She smiled back in a way I hadn't seen before. It was almost like we were more connected in that moment, and I couldn't stop looking into her eyes. They stared down at me like pools of endless night.

"What are you two talking about?" Liza said, and we both ignored her. Liza could be needy and whiny at times. We both knew to ignore her whenever she got like this. "Seriously, why are you two talking in some kind of code language?"

I laughed. "Even if we tried to explain it to you, Liza, you wouldn't understand."

"So I'm too stupid to catch on, is that what you're saying, Stephen Wilkes?"

I didn't respond and turned my eyes back to Trish. "And what about you?" I asked her. "Has your dad come back yet?"

"No," she said, her tone deadening. "He hasn't, and she just keeps getting worse. We went to this painting class out in Holt together last night, and she kept second-guessing everything she did. We ended up staying there until they closed so she could re-do the painting she'd already spent three hours on. It was really embarrassing."

"Your dad's gone?" Liza said. "Why didn't you tell me, and who's *she*?"

"A classic sign of depression," I said. "She's doubting everything she does."

"We're talking about my mom," Trish told Liza. "And my dad hasn't gone anywhere except for inside himself."

"So what," Liza said, "you two tell each other secrets now that I'm not allowed to know? I'm sick of this shit. You two have been in your own world all week. Don't think I haven't noticed the dopey-eyed looks you've been giving one another."

"Stop overreacting," I snapped. "You can be so needy sometimes, Liza. We've been walking home together, that's all. No need to start acting like we're dating or something."

I couldn't believe the words were there, but I'd said them. And they were still lingering in the atmosphere. I'd imagined what my life might be like if Trish were my girlfriend, and in my imagination it seemed like the best thing ever. But crushing on Trish, which I was finally admitting to myself, didn't mean we were going to start dating. Trish had a lot of other guys in school who were interested. Why would she pick me? But what I'd just said didn't go over lightly. I wasn't sure what had made them both so upset, but they were livid. Liza stormed off to the bathroom, and Trish turned away from me and chewed on her fingernails. She'd given up that habit over the summer when she found her confidence.

The movie kept playing, and I didn't know what to

do. Trish's mom had already brought back the pizza and snacks only to leave again, saying she was going out for dinner with a friend. I decided to try with Trish first. I got up from the floor and sat next to her on the couch.

"Not now, Stephen," she said. "I really, really don't want to talk to you." She held up both her hands in front of her, asking me not to come any closer. "You should go check on Liza—apologize for screaming at her."

"I didn't mean to scream at her…"

"Go apologize," Trish said through her teeth. She never raised her voice. I couldn't think of what I'd done to make her so mad, and I didn't know how to fix something like this. We were getting complicated. I got up from the couch without another word and banged on the bathroom door to get Liza's attention. I heard her sniffling.

"Can I come in?" I asked, and she said that I could. "Look, I'm sorry, Liza. You're not needy. I don't know why I said that. And I shouldn't have talked to you like that. I just don't want you to think we're exiling you from our friendship. You both are my best friends."

"I know." She sucked in air through her nose. "It's not just that. I feel like everyone's been ignoring me lately. Not just you and Trish, but my mom too. I've been trying so hard with ballet, the piano, even tutoring, and she still treats me like I don't exist. It's almost like no matter how hard I try she's still unhappy. I don't feel like I'm good enough for anything anymore."

"You're good enough for everything," I told her. "Your mom is really unhappy. I know I don't know much about it her, but she's always scowling and you're always smiling. Don't let her sad taint your happy. Let her be misera-ble by herself."

"But I want her to be happy," Liza said. "I want her to love me."

"She loves you. She just might not be the best at showing it."

"Well, do you think I just need to keep trying hard to impress her, and then she'll pay more attention to me?"

There wasn't a good answer to her question, as I didn't think her mom would ever give her more attention. Liza's mom was selfish. She used to be a model, she didn't know where Liza's dad was, and she pretended not to care. My mom had told me that she did care, though, and she was ashamed of that fact. I didn't know if that was true, so I said this, "Look, don't worry about trying to impress your mom. She loves you no matter what." And I wasn't sure if that was true either, but I wanted it to be. It made Liza smile, and that was all that really mattered.

"Everything okay now?" Trish asked as we walked back into her family room.

"It's great," said Liza. "I shouldn't have overreacted. It wasn't about you two really."

We all sat down on the couch together, me in the mid-dle, and I leaned over to Trish to whisper in her ear. "I'm sorry for whatever I did to hurt you." She smiled back, but it wasn't the same. Her eyes looked wet, but there were no tears there.

Liza threw a pillow at us. "You two are going to drive me crazy," she said. Trish grabbed another pillow and threw it back. It smacked Liza in her face, and for a second I thought she was going to flip out. Her face stayed calm, too calm, but she just burst into one of her usual fits of laughter. Then we all started laughing. It warmed me from the inside out, but it didn't feel like fire, just heat. And we watched as both the floor lamps began to flicker—off and on, off and on so quickly the lights hummed. The flickering light led to questions, and I was strong enough to try and show them again. I managed to make the TV remote jump into my hand.

"That's insane," Liza said. "Let us see something else!"

CHAPTER 8

# JUST TALKING

THAT NIGHT, WHILE we sat in front of Trish's too big television, I told her and Liza everything that had gone on in the clearing, and all the strange things that had happened since that night. Everything except seeing my mom's reflection, which might have freaked them out. Seeing ghosts was a clear sign of grief, and it wasn't something I was ready to share with anyone. But they believed the rest of the story, and it was only because I had proof this time.

"But what does it mean?" Liza asked. "Can you control it?"

"I couldn't at first, but I've gotten better the more I practice." I was talking too fast again. "I'm not sure what it means. When it first started it only happened whenever I got angry, but now it's like I just need a strong emotion to fuel it. I have to feel something deeply, and then I feel more in touch with the rest of me. It sounds crazy."

"No," Trish said, beaming at me. "It sounds wonderful."

We stayed up until 4 AM, watching TV, making jokes, and eating snacks. Trish's mom let Liza and I stay there for the night because of the time. Liza fell asleep first, and Trish and I put toothpaste on her fingers so she'd coat herself in it as she slept. We forgot that Liza sleeps like a log, and she didn't move or touch her face at all that night. I asked Trish to stay up with me and watch the sunrise, but she fell asleep. My eyes were the last to close, and I stayed awake watching the sun touch the horizon from the floor of Trish's living room. My mom always woke up early just to drink coffee and watch the sunrise from across Lake Jordan. You couldn't see the lake from Trish's house, but I still felt closer to my mom that morning.

Later on that day, after Trish's mom drove us to school, I went to visit the school counselor. After all, it was just talking. Talking wouldn't hurt, but still I didn't want the whole school to know about it. No one wanted to get caught visiting the counselor. It meant one of two things: you were either crazy or desperate for attention. I never paid attention to that sort of the thing, but it was almost like there was some random kid who hid all over the school and took a tally of all the uncool things anyone ever did. So I felt the need to be discreet as I walked to the school's basement. It took going down three flights of stairs and four long adjacent hallways before I stood outside the door of our super-strange guidance counselor, Barry Patterson.

Barry Patterson was one of those teachers who you knew smoked too much pot in college. He took his time when he spoke, as if every word mattered. He was tall, too tall. I hoped I wouldn't be that tall when I got older. His dark, long hair was always pulled back into a ponytail at the nape of his neck, and his crammed office smelled like plastic and aftershave.

When I walked in, I noticed he had a pile of water bottles stashed in a corner. Stacks and stacks of newspaper clippings touched the ceiling. Manila folders, three-ring binders, and loose sheets of blank paper cluttered his desk. Several leather journals lay at his side. It was lunchtime on a Friday, and he was sitting at his desk eating a tray of sushi. I wondered where he bought his groceries from, because I'd never seen anything like it, and I did our grocery shopping. Uncle Kasey refused to do anything even slightly related to the feminine.

"Hey there, Stephen," he said when I walked in holding my backpack by one strap. He knew my name. I'm not sure why it shocked me; all the teachers knew my name. I was supposed to be the fragile kid with the limp and the dead mom. I didn't know how to be that kid. I pulled the strap further up on my shoulder, staring at him. "How's it going, man?" Mr. Patterson asked. I still stood there not moving and not saying anything. He stayed silent, waiting for my next move. He kept staring, trying to meet my eyes, but I wasn't ready to give anything away.

And somehow I found my voice. "Fine," I muttered with an unnecessary hand gesture.

"Well, have a seat, have a seat, my man. I'm so glad you came by to see me. Everything alright? Something you need to talk about?"

I sat down, staring at the floor. "No, no uh… Everything's great." The words came out in a whisper so low that I couldn't even hear myself. Barry Patterson looked confused.

"Well, I don't know if you know this, Stephen, but people only come down here when they need someone to talk to, about something they don't want to talk about. Do you have a lot of things you don't want to talk about?"

I nodded and dropped my backpack on the floor. I didn't know if I could do this. Talking about everything seemed like the worst idea ever. It wasn't going to change anything; things were going to stay the same. But Mr. Patterson didn't look upset or agitated with my loss for words. He just stared, trying to look supportive, but his smile was too big. He had horse-teeth with yellowish-brown stains from drinking too much coffee.

"Why don't we start with making a list of all the things you don't want to talk about?" He opened a drawer in his desk and pulled out a notepad and blue ink pen. He scribbled the date at the top, and I stared at the dark hair on his knuckles.

"What do you mean?"

"You came here for a reason, Stephen. It is Stephen, right?" I nodded, and he jotted my name down. "You came here because someone thinks you need to talk to me, I'm sure. So let's make a list so I know what you want to discuss and what you don't."

That seemed more than fair to me. "Well, for starters," I said and grabbed a multi-colored high-lighter from his desk. It was shaped like a triangle, and I fidgeted with it to keep myself talking. "I don't want to talk about my mom's death, my dad, or my crazy uncle."

"That's a lot to not want to talk about. Any reason why you don't want to talk about those things?" he asked, looking me in the eyes. When most adults looked me in the eyes, I couldn't make eye contact with them, but with Barry Patterson it was easy. He didn't act like I expected an adult to act. He wasn't high-strung.

I shrugged. "I don't know," I said. "I guess I don't want to talk about that stuff because everyone expects to me to talk about it, and I'm just not ready."

"That makes complete sense to me," Mr. Patterson said, stowing his lunch away in a nearby trash can. He wiped his mouth on the sleeve of his light blue button-up shirt. "Is there anything that you do want to talk about?"

I thought for a second, and I knew that Barry wouldn't ever repeat anything I said. I'd only just met him, but I knew I could trust him. He was *that* guy. Barry was that guy who only talked when it added to the conversation. He didn't speak to fill the empty spaces between people. He liked watching them squirm, but not kids. He liked kids, which was easy to tell by the way he had smiled when I walked through the door. And for all of those various reasons, I gave him a bit of the truth. "I think I'd like to talk about what makes a marriage work, and how to deal with people who are trying to destroy their own lives."

"Are you trying to destroy your life by getting married?"

I laughed at his awkward, pessimistic joke, knowing that he probably had a wife he loved. "My parents are gone," I told him just so he would know where I was coming from. "My mom's dead, and my dad couldn't handle it, so he left. And I don't know, I just would like to be able to understand them better."

"Why do you care about understanding your parents?" he asked.

"I don't want to make the same mistakes as them," I said. "I just want to know where it all went wrong, and then maybe I'll be able to stop hating them."

"Your parents were divorced?"

"No, they weren't divorced."

"So what went wrong, then?"

Everything had gone wrong. My mom hated herself; she cheated on my dad. And all my dad ever did was stay, wallowing in sorrow, hanging on to her every word. I couldn't say anything else about their marriage. Barry sensed that and decided to move on.

"Who do you know who's trying to destroy their lives?"

"Well, my uncle, but his is already ruined, so…"

"And you've already said that you don't want to talk about him, so let's not."

"Right, well, my little brother, he's starting to act like a complete little shit, like he wants to be a bully or something. He's been skipping school and hockey practice, and he won't listen to anything I have to say. I mean, I know it's just because of everything that's going on, but I'm afraid he's going to make this big mistake that he can't undo."

"And exactly how old is he?"

"He's twelve, but he'll be thirteen next month. There's only like a year and a few months between us," I said. "But I'm still older. It's my job to protect him, but he won't let me."

"Look out for him because you love him," he said.

"But he's only twelve. I doubt he's going to make a mistake he can't undo. You shouldn't be the one protecting him anyway. Doesn't your uncle watch over you guys?"

"He lives with us," I said. "But he doesn't watch over us."

"Let me guess," he asked without really asking, "you're more of the adult now—you watch out for your little brother and take care of stuff around the house. You do what your uncle should probably be doing?"

I nodded.

"Well, Stephen, you need to stop doing those things. You're just a kid, and it's not your job to be the parent or housekeeper."

"But if I don't do it, who will?" I asked.

"You can't be responsible for everyone. You can only take care of yourself."

Barry made it sound so simple, but it wouldn't be that easy. With both my mom and dad gone, I had to be the one. I didn't get a choice.

# EVERYONE LOVES A CHALLENGE

A MONTH PASSED SINCE that first conversation with Barry, and I continued to see him at least once a week. Talking to him helped. We never went too deep. It was just nice sharing my stresses and all my worries. I wanted to be someone. I wanted a future, but lately I couldn't focus. Barry helped me regain that focus.

It was easy to pinpoint what mattered to me in life when I talked to him. Like, I didn't care about fitting in, and he got that. Most adults didn't understand my reasoning, not even my mom had understood. But he did. Barry never asked about the things I didn't want to talk about, and that helped even more. Barry Patterson was my cool adult friend who listened to all my adolescent tripe. I'm not sure why he was so willing, of course it was his job to listen, but he really seemed to care about whether I lived or died, succeeded or failed. It mattered to him. And that made me feel a hell of a lot better about myself.

"When you fit in with all the others," Barry said one Thursday after school. It was already November, and all the leaves had fallen weeks ago. The cold had settled in like a wet puzzle piece. "It's easy to lose yourself. You have to remember what means the most to you, what you value, and you won't care about what others think."

"But what if I want to care about what others think?" I asked, shifting in my chair so that I was sitting on my hands. Barry was helping me to break my habit of talking with my hands. It was a ritual I wanted to end because it increased my anxiety.

"Worrying too much about what others think will make you unhappy," he told me. "You get one life, just one, and you'd better spend it on the things that matter to you, or else you'll be miserable. And I'm not saying that people will never understand you, because there are those who do, but worrying about pleasing them is nothing but a distraction from your own wants."

"So what should I do about Trish?" I asked. "I definitely care what she thinks."

"Does she know how much you care?"

I laughed. "Definitely not," I said. "I don't want her to know; she'll just reject me."

"If you've already decided you're not good enough for her, then why waste your time?" he asked me.

"What do you mean?"

"I mean you're already putting yourself down and you don't even know how she feels yet. You're writing yourself off completely because of self-doubt." He paused, trying to get me to understand. "People are going to put you down your whole life," Barry said. "There's no reason for you to put yourself down too. Give her a chance to say no; don't make the decision for her because you're scared."

"So you're saying I should ask her out? I should let her tell me no, instead of just assuming that she wouldn't pick me?"

"Exactly," he said. "You've got to stop getting down on yourself. You are worthy of all the things you want. Just because you had some bad things happen doesn't mean you've become a less worthwhile person. It actually makes you more of a worthwhile one."

"How so?"

"Well, now you have interesting stories to tell. You have an obstacle to overcome, and you will overcome it."

"But how can I overcome this?" I asked. "It's almost like all my emotions are swallowing me whole. I don't know what I'm doing anymore."

"You just have to try. If you keep trying, it will happen. I promise."

I spent the rest of that evening mulling over Barry's words as I lay in bed. My uncle hadn't been home in three nights, but I was teaching myself not to care—to ignore his putdowns and threats. The last night he'd come home I'd woken to him beating me senseless. I lifted my shirt and could still see the lengthy bruise that stretched across my torso. The bruise left a stinging in my limbs, a reminder that my uncle needed to leave this house for good. If he wanted to drink himself into oblivion, there wasn't a thing I could do to stop him. He didn't like me, and that wasn't going to change. And why should I care if he liked me or not? My uncle didn't matter. Everything Barry said was right; it all made perfect sense. If only Warren could hear the stuff Barry said. I had thought about bringing in a voice recorder, but knew better. Warren would have just used the fact that I was seeing the counselor to blackmail me.

Things with Warren had only gotten worse. He rarely showed up to school and when he did he left halfway through the school day, heading to one of the old abandoned warehouses with Jared. Trish said her mom asked why she saw Warren there during school hours. Warren had stopped going to hockey practice, and I knew that was why he had so much pent-up aggression. He had moved from tormenting the other kids to torturing them. Liza learned that Sam the Man had moved across town. His mom really had lost her marbles and was staying in a mental institution in Detroit. Liza felt like that was what had made Warren shut down. There was no one left to care about him, and he'd convinced himself that I didn't matter anymore. He wouldn't talk to anyone except for Jared, and I was sure that their conversations couldn't be all that meaningful.

Barry told me that the only way to help Warren was to take care of myself first, and then lead by example. That was one thing I wasn't sure if he was right about. Warren didn't admire me or look up to me. I always did the right thing, and it hadn't affected him yet. But I decided to trust Barry. Maybe he knew something I didn't.

It was the beginning of November, and the fair was in town. Tomorrow was Friday, and I decided that it was the perfect time to ask Trish out. I rolled over in my bed and stared out at Lake Jordan in the dead of night. Of course I was scared to ask her, and that wouldn't change, but I wanted to know if she liked me. I felt like I had to know or I was going to go insane. She always saw right through me, so I knew that if I tried to downplay the way I felt, she'd know. Trish was still pissed about what I'd said at movie night, although she wouldn't admit that to me. I still didn't understand her anger, and I hadn't asked about it either. She'd kept her distance from me, and now was the time to break down the walls of awkwardness.

When I walked into homeroom that morning, Trish sat in her usual desk at the front of the class. There were no classes or learning in homeroom, but Trish always sat up front no matter what. She was the brain, the overachiever, a total nerd, and that was one of the things I liked most about her. She cared about people, without meaning to, and she was brilliant. Maybe even smarter than me, but we had our strengths and weaknesses.

Trish was awesome at English and Social Studies, while it was Math and Science that I excelled at. Liza did her own thing. She was a bit above average when it came to schoolwork, but she outshined us both when it came to music and the arts. Liza was a ballerina. She wasn't sitting up front with Trish, so she must have been running late to school. Her mom never cared about her absences or tardiness. I'd never seen anyone dance like Liza, though. She became the music when she danced. Liza had a recital on Sunday, and we both promised to be there. She'd returned to her usual annoying ways within the past month, but I worried what she might think of me asking Trish to go alone with me to the fair. It was kind of a blessing in disguise that she wasn't there this morning.

"Good morning," I said to Trish with a smug grin wearing away at my features.

"Hey," she replied, not looking up from her book.

"What are you reading?" I asked as I sat down. I put my backpack in my lap, preparing to rush out the door once the first period bell rang. She shrugged, and it dawned on me that this was going to be even harder than I had imagined.

"Look, Trish," I said, sounding demanding. She liked it when I was more confident, and so I would try for her, just to get her attention. "Are you pissed at me about something?"

"Why would I be pissed at you?" The way she said *you* made me feel like a non-issue. It was almost like I meant so little to her that I couldn't cause her to react to anything, ever. Well, she was going to give me some kind of reaction today.

"I know I did something to make you mad, and I don't know what it is, but I'm sorry, Trish. I really am," I said, but she still refused to turn and look at me. "How much longer are you going to keep ignoring me?"

"As long as it takes for you to get the message."

"And what message is that?" I asked.

"That you can't just say mean things to hurt people and then expect them to not be hurt!"

"What did I say?"

"It's nothing. I don't want to talk about it."

"It's not nothing, Trish!" I shouted, and the class shushed me. I leaned in over her shoulder to whisper in her ear. Her smell overwhelmed me, but I kept my focus. "I can't read your mind. Please just tell me what's bothering you so I can fix it." No response. "Will you go to the fair with me tonight?" I asked, letting the air rush out of my lungs. Trish turned around to face me, but there was a scowl on her pretty face. She was going to say no. She hated me, and now she was going to let me have it.

"You're asking me out?" she said, and I nodded, refusing to break eye contact with her. I wanted her to feel just how serious I was. "Why should I go out with you, Stephen? It's not like I matter to you at all. You said so yourself."

"When did I say that?"

"You don't like me. I don't mean anything to you."

"Trish, you're my best friend. You mean everything to me, and you know that."

I didn't hear the bell ring this time, but everyone started filing out of the classroom door. Liza still wasn't in school. She never skipped, so I found it strange. She'd been coming in late, though, because of late-night dance practices. Trish and I walked down the hall. I was probably too close to her. I should have given her some space, but I couldn't. She hadn't said "no," but she also hadn't said "yes" either.

"You told Liza not to worry about us getting close," she breathed. I could hear tears caught in her throat. "You said that it wasn't like we were going to start dating."

And that shocked the hell out of me. "Are you saying you want to start dating?"

"No," she shouted, stopping in the hall. "That's not what I meant at all. I just think that before you make it clear there's nothing going on between us, you should ask me how I feel. Or just be more sensitive about it. You didn't even consider that I might have a crush on you."

God, she was so mature—too mature for me. Or maybe we were that perfect match: two kids born as adults. Adults that could only function as children.

"Do you have a crush on me?" I asked. I could feel my lips curling into a smile. Something in my head told me to fight the warmth I was feeling, but I ignored it. She stared at me, and I didn't turn away. This felt completely right.

"No," Trish said. "I don't have a crush on you. Maybe there was a time when I thought about you too much, but now I see that you don't care about me, so why should I bother."

She still cared. Trish still cared in a very big way, and for once I was catching on to all of her clues. She wanted me to take the lead. "Can we just forget about what I said to Liza?" I asked her. "It was a dumb thing to say, and it was super inconsiderate, so I just want to move on. Let's go to the fair, okay?"

She was silent, thinking. My eyes searched her face, trying to read her mind. "Alright, I'll go," she said. "But I'm not promising to be pleasant to you, Stephen Wilkes."

The way Trish said my name echoed through my ears the entire day. I couldn't get her smile or those dark brown eyes out of my head. She'd said yes to me, and even though Warren had tried starting a fight with me at lunch, I couldn't care less. All that mattered was what mattered to me, and that was selfish, but I needed that bit of selfishness right now.

It surprised me to see him and Jared even in school.

Warren looked like a sloth, like a sleazy ball of lazy slime as I stared across the cafeteria at him. I watched as he and Jared took turns pouring milk down the backs of sixth-graders. Warren stood there looking like Uncle Kasey, wearing Jared's angry face and doing his haughty laugh. I tried to block it out, but it couldn't be done. We still weren't talking. Most nights he went straight to his room, and I'd stopped trying to force him to eat dinner. He wouldn't listen to me.

Warren caught me staring and flipped me off. I turned back to Trish and Liza who were both finished eating. He was a lost cause. I didn't know why I was watching him so closely.

"Where were you this morning?" I asked Liza. She was studying for a test we had in science class. Last minute studying was becoming a part of her routine.

"My mom was running late this morning. Practice ran late last night, so she let me sleep in. I didn't even get a chance to study or do any homework."

Warren walked over to our table, and I opened my mouth to say something to him. But then I closed it shut when I saw him reach for Liza's book and toss it across the cafeteria. He laughed and started to walk away.

"Little jerk," Trish said as she got up to grab Liza's book. Liza sat there with shock bleeding out of her ears. Trish picked up the book, and Warren knocked it out of her hands.

"Leave it there," he commanded Trish. "Let your little loser friend come and get it." Trish ignored him and pushed past him to pick up the book once again. And I watched as Warren bumped into her, knocking her onto the floor. He stared down at her, mocking, then turned to see if Jared was laughing, if he'd earned his approval. Jared laughed, and Warren laughed only after receiving Jared's confirmation of his actions.

This was my cue. The stage beckoned me. I stood up slowly, trying to create more tension in the already silent cafeteria. "Leave her alone, Warren," I said.

"Why?" he asked, his voice filled with a challenge. "Worried I'll hurt one of your little girlfriends? Give it up. We all know you're a coward. You're an even bigger coward than Dad. At least he knew his place."

I left the table and walked over to where Trish sat and Warren stood. He wanted me to look at him, but I wouldn't. I grabbed Trish by her tiny wrist and helped her up from the cafeteria floor. Everyone went back to eating their lunch, but Warren wasn't finished.

"Why don't you just kill yourself, you fucking cripple? No one cares if you live or die."

That one hurt, but I wasn't going to let him see it. "Let it go, Warren," I said. "Whatever you're holding on to that's making me out to be the enemy, just let it go. I'm not Dad."

"What would your mom say if she heard you say something like that?" Trish demanded of Warren. Her words almost managed to change his expression. I could see his face softening, a bit of the hurt fading.

"Shut up, you black bitch. No one cares what you think."

Warren couldn't take back what he'd just said, and I knew I wouldn't ever be able to forget it. I heard Trish's voice catch. She was going to cry, and I wasn't going to let

Warren get away with hurting her like that. I didn't spend any more time wondering what had made him so evil. I lunged across the cafeteria, grasping for his throat. My arms caught his shoulders, and I pulled his face to mine.

"Stephen."

I turned around to see Barry Patterson standing there. I let go of Warren and ran my hands along the pockets of my jeans. I needed to place myself if I was going to let go of my anger.

"Is something going on here?" Barry asked Warren.

"Nope, not a thing," Warren said, glaring me down. "Just family stuff."

## CHAPTER 10

# A FAIR TO REMEMBER

TRISH AND I didn't mention the incident in the cafeteria as we walked home that day, but I noticed her fingers shaking whenever she pulled on the ends of her hair. What Warren had said didn't seem to bother her as much as it bothered me. I wanted to ask her about it, but I also didn't want to kill the mood. She'd agreed to be alone with me at one of our town's most sacred events. Lake Odessa didn't have much, but the fall festival near town square was one of the best in Michigan. We had a Ferris wheel, bumper cars, and even a space-walk. It was just about the coolest thing that happened around this time of year—except for the living nativity scene, but that was more watching, less doing. There was a sharp pinch in my chest as I remembered my mom wouldn't be here to see it this year. It was one of her favorite things to do, ever. And this would be the first year my family wouldn't stand together all bundled up outside the

Presbyterian Church of Christ waiting to get a glimpse of little baby Jesus.

When we got to Trish's house, her dad was home. She told me he usually tried to come home early on Fridays because he spent most of the week in Detroit. Trish asked him if he would drive us out to the fair. It would have been too long of a walk in the darkness.

"It's good to see you, kid!" Mr. Adams said, pulling me into a hug. I hadn't expected her dad to seem like himself anymore, given just how much Trish's mom had changed. Her dad must have been living off the happiness her mom had let go.

"Good to see you too, Mr. Adams," I said, rubbing my ribcage. He'd almost crushed it.

"Going out to the fair tonight, huh? That sounds like a lot of fun." He mused as we told him our plans. "Where's your mom, Trish?"

"I'm not sure," Trish replied. "She's probably out shopping. Did you try calling her?"

He didn't respond. "You kids ready to go?" he asked. I didn't know what he was playing at, but he was putting on the exact same front my dad had before my mom died. Everything he said was way too sweet, well beyond endearing. He was hiding something, but I guessed most adults were hiding something.

We piled into Mr. Adams' brand new Audi. Well, brand new to his family. It was a used car, but it smelled new. People stared at us as we drove across town in the shiny, expensive, and somewhat new vehicle. My palms were sweating, and I only managed to glance at Trish a few times during the car ride. There was no way to know what she was thinking, but I hoped she was just as nervous as I was. Her dad went on and on about his new job as if it mattered to us. Mr. Adams was just as oblivious as Mrs. Adams. They had forgotten that their daughter needed them to be alright for her sake. Watching it all play out made me appreciate just how good of actors my parents had been. But maybe Trish didn't know what to pay attention to. Maybe I only saw it now because I knew what to look for.

The line for admission only stretched about halfway down Abbots Road. Trish's dad dropped us off at the entrance gate and handed Trish several bills. I hadn't thought of how we would pay for things. I didn't have much money, but I didn't want Trish to pay for everything. That wouldn't help her like me. The little bit of money I did have, I'd saved up from cutting lawns over the summer. There was enough for me to buy my ticket, and hopefully enough to win Trish a big stuffed animal. I wasn't sure if she wanted a big stuffed animal, but I was going off of what I'd seen in movies. If this night were going to be anything like the movies, then Trish would want a big stuffed animal.

The wind whipped all around us as we walked in, and those familiar carnival sounds rang in our ears—bells and whistles, chimes and dings, and that annoying circus song that always played in the background. Stands for fried butter, fried Oreos, and even fried bananas—an actual fruit—cluttered the walkways. The crowds made it difficult to get to the rides we wanted, but it wasn't dark yet. The sun lingered, leaving pink and purple hues in the sky. The tilt-a-whirl stood surrounded by people, against the darkening gray sky. Trish wrapped her fingers around my own. I didn't ruin it by looking back at her, willing her into self-consciousness. Instead, I grabbed her hand and pulled her close as if I was shielding her from the wind, but I just wanted her body close to mine. She laughed as I pulled her along the road filled with neon signs touting pizza and cotton candy for sale.

"Are you hungry?" I asked Trish as we took in our surroundings.

"Not really," she said. "But I do want a candy apple. Let's stop at the sweets store before we leave?" She was asking rather than telling, but I didn't respond, and so it turned her question into a command. I wanted her to feel strong after what Warren had said.

We played games and rode most of the rides as the fair lights glowed. Sadness stayed away in this place. It was easy to make new memories, and this night wouldn't be one I would ever forget. Trish bought us each a slice of pizza, and we sat at the metal tables next to the water gun horse race. We'd just finished riding bumper cars, and we'd both been attacked by a swarm of elementary school kids who were here for a birthday party. Trish watched the sky, staring up at the night clouds and sparkling stars.

"I started seeing the counselor," I said to get her attention.

"Is it helping?"

I shrugged. "Have you met the counselor?" Trish told me that she hadn't met him, but she'd gone with Liza once to see him. She explained how she had waited outside the door while Liza went in to discuss a really big secret that she refused to talk about. "I thought you two told each other everything?" I asked.

"We do. I don't really know if it was a secret, or just something to do with her mom. I think she's dating this new guy and has been leaving Liza home alone."

"Poor Liza," I said. "Her mom better be at this recital, or Liza's going to lose it."

"You still haven't answered my question," Trish reminded me.

"Is it helping?" I asked for a confirmation. She nodded. "Yeah, I would say it is definitely helping. I mean, I don't go there to talk about my mom or my uncle. But it helps with the day-to-day, and that's all I can focus on right now."

"So you're going there all the time now, but you're not talking about the things that are affecting you the most? That sounds real smart." Her tone was sarcastic.

"Whatever, Trish," I said, offended. "I wouldn't expect you to understand anyway."

"What's that supposed to mean?" she snapped.

"It means what it means. Both your parents are still living. Your life hasn't changed. You don't know what it's like for me right now, so be nicer, okay?"

That pissed her off. She got up from the table, moving away from me, but she held my eyes in place. I wasn't even upset. Her heated expression mesmerized me.

"Come on, Trish," I shouted after her. "You can't expect me to not get upset when you're basically telling me how I should be handling this. I shouldn't have said you don't understand, but you can't automatically assume that you do either." She walked back toward the table.

"You're right," she breathed. "I don't know what it's like for you, but I wish you would tell me what it's like. I want to know how you're feeling, and you won't ever tell me." She paused, chewed on the fingernail on her ring finger, and put her other hand on her hip. "Why did you ask me here tonight without Liza? I want the truth."

I wanted to put the blame back on her, and accuse her of liking me too, without saying anything. But that's what a coward would have done. "Because I like spending time with you, Trish. It's nice when it's just the two of us."

"So you don't want Liza hanging out with us anymore?"

"No, not like that. You and Liza are both my best friends, but..." I took a deep breath. "But I care about you in a different way than I care about Liza, I think."

"You think?"

"Well, yeah," I said. "I'm not completely sure what this is I'm feeling about you, and I just want us to hang out is all. But at the same time I don't want things to change. It's hard."

"It is hard," she admitted. "I've wanted to tell you the same thing, but I don't want Liza to be upset. I want everything to stay the same, so I've been ignoring my thoughts about you." She smiled at me and then looked away. "But I'm not sure if I can, even for Liza's sake. She's had a crush on you since we were seven, and I always thought you'd pick her if you ever liked one of us."

"Liza's like my sister. Why would I pick her?" She shrugged. "Just tell me what it is, Trish."

"I don't know why you act like you don't see it." She cast her eyes down and sat on the bench across from me.

"I'm the only black person in town, Stephen. Unless I go outside the city, dating isn't going to be very easy for me once we get to high school."

"You think I'd pick Liza over you because of your skin? I'm not that shallow, Trish."

"It's not about being shallow. It's about going with what people expect, and what you're used to. Most people cling to what's familiar."

"People who think like that *are* shallow. That's completely ignorant, Trish. It's stupid, and I don't think that way."

"I know you don't," she said. "Liza doesn't either. But unfortunately most people in this town do. This is something you wouldn't understand," she told me. "So please don't even try. I don't want to talk about this."

"We don't have to," I said, understanding without completely understanding. Trish felt different, like an outsider. It wasn't something she had decided to feel, but something others had forced upon her. That much made sense to me, but crushes still didn't.

"I can't believe Liza has a crush on me. Why didn't she ever say anything?"

"She doesn't anymore," Trish said. "It really was a long time ago. She's regained her senses now, but I haven't." She actually sounded disappointed. "It's just the rule with girls, you know. She saw you first."

I didn't even think I had a shot at getting one girl to like me, let alone my two best friends. Then I remembered how immature the other guys in our classes were. I thought about how Coleman always smelled like feet, and how Ralph had stapled his hand to a piece of paper last week in Science.

We ended it there and walked around the fair a bit more. Trish continued to let me pull her close, and our body warmth made it less cold. A familiar heat overtook me. I felt like I was swimming through a warm spring. Trish smiled at me and laughed at all of my old jokes. It made me think of the photos I'd seen of my parents when they went to the fair together back in high school. I wondered if our smiles would last longer than theirs had. The sun set, and moonlight mixed with carnival lights took over the dark sky. The night grew colder, and I held Trish just a little bit tighter, a little bit closer. It made me feel strong to protect her from the wind. I couldn't stop staring into her eyes. I could see my upside-down reflection around her irises. She was seeing me. I pulled her close once more and kissed the top of her hair. She laughed. It was the most amazing sound, on the absolute best night of my life.

"I want to win something for you," I told her.

"Trying to show off your manliness?" she questioned. "It's sweet of you, but I don't really want anything. Those games are traps anyway; you'll end up spending all of your money."

"Just let me do this, okay?" I said and walked her back over to the water gun horse race.

"You can try all you want, but I refuse to be impressed by a giant stuffed animal."

She'd be impressed. I'd been practicing my moving of objects for weeks now. It got easier with each attempt, and I'd learned to levitate things around me with little effort.

I wanted to win the horse race on my own, though, so I tried several times, and each time I failed I tried again. My money was almost spent, and if I kept going at this rate I wouldn't have enough money to buy Trish the candy apple she wanted. Nothing else mattered except captivating her. I motioned for her to sit in the spinning stool next to mine.

"It's alright to give up, Stephen," she said to me. "I already told you I don't really want one. I don't even like stuffed animals."

"Just watch," I said. The acne-faced teenager who stood behind the control station announced that another race was about to start. And instead of using the trigger of the gun to shoot water at the moving horse, I used my mind. The water shot out like a bullet and powered the toy horse to the end of the race. The winning alarm sounded, and I made the lights heat up, bursting into little sparkles of fire, like fireworks. Trish knew I had used my mind, and she looked at me laughing. I stared back at her, and she pressed her lips to mine, and I knew that she meant it. I knew that it was real, this thing with her. I was feeling it all too deeply.

Trish picked the biggest unicorn they had. It was light purple, with a sparkly horn on its head. The unicorn's mane looked like pink cotton candy, but Trish loved it despite its fantastical appearance. She held it close and kept saying it was the coolest thing ever, and that I'd acquired it in the coolest way ever.

"I thought you hated stuffed animals?" I asked her.

"Not this one," she said. "This one is perfect." She looked up at me and planted a kiss on my cheek. She was proud of my difference. I wanted her to be just as proud of her own.

Trish munched on her candy apple while we stood outside waiting on her dad to pick us up. He was already an hour late. "He'll be here," she reasoned with herself rather than me. We used a payphone to call her house, but no one answered. I told her we should walk home, just in case her dad had fallen asleep on the couch or something. She was slow to accept my suggestion, but she gave in once the cold started to cut through our clothes. I thought she might be worried about him, but she wasn't thinking about him at all.

"You don't plan things out as much as you used to," Trish said, and I asked her what she meant. "This whole trip to the fair," she pondered. "It was so spur-of-the-moment. I'm just used to seeing you map out routes whenever we even go to the shopping center. You're changing, Stephen," she breathed. "You just don't know it yet."

She kissed me again once we reached her house. I couldn't stop breathing her into my soul. We really were too young to be this obsessed with each other. I knew that it was going to change things, but I didn't want to tarnish the moment by acting like I normally would. I wanted to be a little reckless, and not consider each possible outcome. So I ignored the future and decided I'd handle everything I was feeling later on.

# CHAPTER 11

# DANCE LIKE A GIRL

AS I WALKED home I couldn't stop sniffing the collar of my jean jacket. It still smelled like Trish. There wasn't a single thing on the planet that could knock me down from the high I was feeling. Trish had kissed me. The one thing I'd been fantasizing about since the start of the school year had actually happened. It didn't feel real. It felt like I was floating, drifting through space and time until my soul would encounter Trish's again. If you had asked me then, I would have told you that Trish's eyes sparkled every time she looked at me. It was meant for me, and I hadn't noticed that before tonight.

Things were going to change. They had to, but I wasn't going to worry about it. We hadn't set any boundaries, and I didn't see any point in it. Trish was my best friend, and I didn't want that to change, but the way we acted around Liza would have to stop. I wasn't going to make Liza feel uncomfortable. My guilt set in. This didn't feel right. I wasn't sure how Liza felt, but I didn't want to ruin the best thing I had going on right now—my friendship with the two of them. Not one, but two. If Trish and I kept this up, would we unintentionally exile Liza? It wasn't worth considering.

When I got home, my uncle's car was parked in our driveway. He'd been staying out so late most nights that I hadn't considered him coming home tonight. Instead of walking through the front door, I decided to sneak in through the back. It wasn't late, maybe 10 o'clock at night, but I was still leery of what might be lurking.

I pressed my ear to the glass of our sliding back door. My uncle's snoring even permeated the door pane. He must have passed out somewhere else because I didn't see him in the hall. I unlocked the back door and stepped inside. My feet crept down the hall, past the kitchen and TV room.

"Where the hell have you been?" Warren's voice called out to me from the kitchen. "No use trying to sneak in here. Your bum leg's going to give you away."

I watched him as he leaned back against the kitchen counter and crossed his right leg over the other. He chewed on a bologna and cheese sandwich, wearing his pajamas and standing in our bright yellow kitchen. He looked comical, but he was trying to be intimidating. I didn't say anything to him. I just stood there, watching, waiting to see what he might say next. He was unpredictable, and I was beginning to embrace it.

"You went out with that nerdy black girl?" Warren asked.

I limped over toward the kitchen. "Why don't you

stop talking about Trish like that? What the hell is wrong with you?"

"What the hell is wrong with *you*? Stop being such a fucking nerd."

He wasn't worth it. I knew that he was just looking for some weak target to take his frustrations out on. But it wouldn't be me. I turned around and headed back toward my room.

"You can fuck off anyway," he said, raising his voice, but still whispering at me. "You and that stupid black bitch. You're useless," he laughed.

I didn't think twice before I took the 11 steps I needed to clear the TV room and head toward the kitchen. My body lunged at Warren, and we collided. He fell to the floor, and I straddled him, punching him again and again. I couldn't stop hitting him. My fists were my only hope to knock some actual sense into him. I kept shouting things at him with each blow. But most of what I was saying didn't make sense. I remember blaming him for Dad leaving. I called him names, mean ones that I think cut too deep.

It's no excuse, but I was pissed. One minute I was floating over all my problems, watching from above. And now I was knee-deep in shit, scuffling on the kitchen floor with my kid brother. This would have made my mom sad. She would have wanted us to get along, but I was pissed with Warren for everything. He was the only person who could understand, and he was refusing to. Or maybe I was refusing to, I wasn't sure. All I could focus on was my anger, and then the light flipped on in the kitchen.

My uncle stood by the light switch smirking, looking

like a bat from hell. Warren had his hands around my neck in a weak attempt to choke me. "Get off me, you freak," he said and then spit in my face. Uncle Kasey walked over and pulled me off Warren.

"Who the hell do you think you are?" he said, not really expecting a response. "There won't be any violence in this house. You're out of here. Hitting Warren like that? I don't know what the hell has gotten into you."

He held me by my jacket collar and hoisted me over to the front door. This overweight crocodile was planning on throwing me out of my own house. I started swinging at him, and knocked him across his jaw. He looked at me and opened the front door, preparing to toss me out into the cold like an unwanted kitten. When he opened the door, we both saw Bethany Way, Elliot's mom, standing on our doorstep.

"What the fuck do you want?" my uncle said.

"I heard shouting and thought I should come over and check on Stephen. Is something wrong?" she asked as her eyes roamed over me and my uncle.

"There are a lot of things wrong!" my uncle shouted.

"Well, why don't you put Stephen down, and we can talk about this calmly."

My uncle shook his head. "There's no need for calm, because I'm throwing him out of this house. He can't get along with Warren, and I just caught him beating up on the poor kid."

"Stephen picking on Warren?" Mrs. Way questioned. "That doesn't make much sense. My daughter's told me that it's always been quite the opposite, and she's been babysitting the boys for years."

"If you want him, then take him because he can't stay here!" my uncle shouted again. "He can't come back until he's learned to get along with Warren. I won't have fighting in this house." My uncle snarled like a rabid dog. I worried he might bite Elliot's mom.

"I will take him!" Mrs. Way shouted. "And I hope you can learn how to treat children. Stephen is a good kid. You're just too drunk to see it."

"You don't know me," Uncle Kasey growled. "You don't get to talk to me like that, you useless wench!"

"Nearly everyone in town has seen you down at that bar by the steel forge drinking too much and starting trouble," Mrs. Way said. "And if you think for one minute that I'm just going to sit back and watch you mistreat these boys then you're mistaken!"

My uncle was wearing his usual mischievous toddler grin, trying to intimidate Mrs. Way. But Bethany Way held her own. She stood her ground, and that pissed my uncle off.

"Your husband should keep you in the house, you fat bitch," Uncle Kasey said. His breath turned to frost in the cold night air, and he stood there breathing in excitement over what he'd just said.

I couldn't control my anger, I wanted to, but couldn't. The familiar heat was building in my chest. The porch light shattered and blew out, and I swung at my uncle. He knocked me down to the ground. Mrs. Way shocked the hell out of me. She didn't break eye contact with my uncle, but somehow she managed to grab me by the hand and tow me across the street to her lawn. She shot my uncle a seething look and then turned to me.

"Are you alright? Did he hurt you?" she asked me, sounding far too much like my own mom, causing a forsaken feeling in my chest.

"I'm fine," I said, throwing my hand up to stop her from inspecting my limbs. We walked through the front door and into her living room.

"Is there anything you need to go back over there for?" she asked me. Mr. Way walked out of his bedroom and stood next her. "Where were you?" she said to him. "I needed you. You should have heard what Kasey just said. It was like being in high school all over again, watching him torture Daisy."

That was my first confirmation that my uncle had been an asshole all his life. It felt good to know that I hadn't been the one to cause the excessive drinking.

"I'm sorry." Mr. Way leaned in and kissed Mrs. Way's forehead. "I was half asleep, and I didn't take you seriously. I didn't think there was anything going on."

"Well, there is!" Bethany Way shouted. "Just look at the bruises all over him. I don't think Warren's being treated as badly." Mrs. Way ran her finger over a bruise on my left cheek. It was weeks old, but she kept examining it. "He needs clothes, David. He can't keep these same clothes on."

"Let's just wait for the night and see if things mellow out. I'm sorry I didn't believe you."

"It doesn't matter," I said. Somehow, I remembered the bracelet. I'd left it in the front pocket of my hoodie since I found it. "Here," I said, handing it to her.

She thanked me, without asking any questions about my parents. I think she could tell it wasn't a good time.

I slept on the couch in the Way's living room that night worrying about Warren. He didn't get it. For whatever reason he believed getting me out of the house would give him some kind of advantage. It didn't occur to him that I acted as his shield. I wouldn't be there anymore as the punching bag. Warren needed me to protect him, even though he didn't know it.

When I woke, Mrs. Way stood in the kitchen behind me making eggs and bacon. It smelled the way Saturdays used to smell at my house. She made her way around the kitchen humming some faraway tune. The food smell reminded me too much of my mom. I rolled over on the couch and turned toward the kitchen to look at Mrs. Way.

"You hungry?" she asked. "A rough night always fades with an amazing breakfast. Do you like pancakes or waffles?"

"Waffles," I said and sat up on the couch to stretch. I'd slept in my clothes and hadn't been as comfortable as I would have liked. I stood up, moving toward their hall bathroom when my eyes caught Elliot sitting at their small island, wearing nothing but a tank top and shorts. She waved at me and smiled, and I took off for the bathroom like a true clown.

We all sat at the table eating breakfast, pretending like the previous night hadn't happened. It didn't bother me. I didn't want to talk about it, so I stayed quiet while Elliot buzzed about homecoming at her school. She wanted to be queen, but some mean girls had nominated her as Ms. Math to play a prank. I tuned most of it out, but managed to hear something about Flint, shopping, and going out for lunch. I sipped on my orange juice and tried not to make eye contact with anyone for longer than a few seconds.

Then I remembered Liza. "Can someone drive me to Liza Martinelli's dance recital tonight?" I asked, and no one said a word. "It's out by the community center near Wilton's?"

Still no words.

"You have to go tonight?" Mrs. Way asked me.

I nodded, gulping down my orange juice. "Yes, tonight's the night. Liza's been practicing for months. She'd kill me if I missed it."

"You two are pretty close, huh?" Elliot asked and nudged my shoulder. I looked at her, and she took a sip of coffee from the burgundy mug in her hands. "She's really cute, Wilkes. I like her a lot." Elliot sounded like a dad granting their approval. I ignored her and turned to Mrs. Way with a plea in my eyes. She would have to drive me.

"Well it sounds wonderful," Mrs. Way said, nodding in my direction. "You can tell Liza we'll be there."

Liza's recital started at six o'clock. Mrs. Way threw my clothes in the wash and let me use the fancy shower in their master bedroom. It wasn't a tub, just a shower—almost like a water closet—but it felt amazing. The water pressure from the showerhead massaged my back and shoulders. What had happened with Warren and my uncle didn't matter. All that mattered was being there for Liza. She needed me.

Elliot and her dad went to her soccer game that evening, instead of riding with us to Liza's dance recital. Mrs. Way drove to the community center before the recital started. I would have wanted to wear something a bit nicer, but I didn't have any choice. We got there about an hour and a half early, which was what I wanted. When we were walking in, I had scanned the parking lot for Ms. Martinelli's car, but it wasn't there. I knew Liza's mom would be late if she decided to come at all, and that Liza had probably walked there on her own. Liza was responsible like that.

When I walked in, there was a line of girls in frilly costumes standing outside the bathroom at the entrance to the community center. The girls fussed over their hair and makeup, and I guessed that those inside the bathroom were putting on their costumes. I assumed Liza was in there with them since she wasn't standing in the line.

Mrs. Way glanced at the line of girls, and I asked her if she would wait for me inside the theatre. She nodded, looking at me as she turned to walk away. Most guys would have felt self-conscious about what I was about to do, but I couldn't. Liza was here all alone. She needed my support. I wanted to be brave enough to walk in on a room filled with pre-teen girls changing, but I wasn't. I stood there frozen, my hand reaching for the door, when Trish walked up.

"You weren't seriously considering going in there alone, were you?" she asked me in a hurried whisper. "You would have embarrassed Liza." She looked at me as if her statement had been common sense. I thought Trish would walk off without me, but she grabbed my hand and pulled me inside the girl's bathroom. My eyes searched the room for Liza, but I didn't see her. "There she is," Trish shouted, pointing to a corner.

Liza sat in a wooden chair pressed up against a wall

near the bathroom stalls. She held her face in her hands, and her shoulders shook with sorrow. We walked up to her without speaking, and Trish put a hand on her shoulder. I watched as Liza looked up at Trish, mascara running down her eyes. I'd never seen Liza in makeup before. It didn't suit her. She was too young; the angles of her face were still too round.

"She's not here," Liza hiccupped, and we both knew just who she was referring to. Trish asked me to grab a tissue. The stalls were full, so I went back out into the chaos, where there was one teenage girl polite enough to hand me a few squares of tissue paper. I handed them to Trish who passed them along to Liza. "She's out on a date with her new boyfriend, and now she's saying she can't make it." Liza hiccupped again.

"How did you get here?" Trish asked Liza.

"I walked," she said. "I thought I might catch the bus, but it was taking too long, and I didn't want to be late." Liza blew her nose. "She knows how much this means to me. I just can't believe it. I might as well be invisible. She doesn't care about me."

"Your mom cares about you," Trish said, wiping tears from Liza's face. "She's just too dumb to realize that you need her right now. But you know what?"

"What?" Liza asked.

"It doesn't matter if she's here, because Stephen and I are here. And we love you, Liza. Completely and totally love you, and we know you're going to be great. You've been practicing non-stop, and tonight's your night, girl!"

"You really think so?"

"For sure," Trish said, taking a makeup brush from

Liza's bright purple bag that had the word "dance" inscribed on it. "You look beautiful."

"I really want to be a ballerina," Liza said, staring at Trish.

"You are a ballerina," Trish said.

Trish dismissed me from the dressing room as she continued her pep talk with Liza. I found my seat next to Mrs. Way that wasn't too far off from the front row. I didn't want to miss a thing. Liza was performing The Nutcracker and had landed the part as the Sugar Plum Fairy. It wasn't the Swan Princess, as Liza had reminded me, but it was still a decent part for someone her age. She was proud, and I was proud of her.

Trish came out and sat beside me. She was quiet and wouldn't look at me. But as Liza took the stage, none of that seemed to matter anymore. We watched her twirl on the balls of her feet. Her tiny pirouettes were like a wonderland as the spotlight reflected off her pale features. Liza looked like magic when she completed her solo. Her grace was beyond anything I'd ever seen, and she poised her body effortlessly. It was like nothing else mattered when Liza danced. This was her way of expressing herself. I got it, and I loved being able to watch her move with such fierce grace. It was her mom's loss. Her mom felt like this new guy was more important than this moment, but I knew there couldn't be anything else that equated to Liza's artfully crafted movements. She looked like a china doll, despite the heavy makeup.

"Stop staring at her," Trish said, nudging me. I hadn't been staring, only appreciating, but I knew she wouldn't understand.

## CHAPTER 12

# THE BREAKING POINT

THAT NEXT MORNING, my uncle still wouldn't let me come home. I wasn't there to witness his words, but when Elliot's mom walked through their front door, it was there in her eyes. She locked eyes with me and shook her head. I knew she'd tried her best, but what did it matter? My bastard of an uncle thought he was running things and that he could kick me out of my very own home. He was a piece of shit, and I would make sure he knew it one of these days. But my returning glance to Elliot's mom expressed none of that. I looked at her then cast my eyes down toward the carpet.

"I'm sorry, Stephen," she mouthed to me. But I wasn't sorry. I was glad to be away from him and Warren for the moment. Uncle Kasey wouldn't take my home, though; that wouldn't happen. He couldn't stake claim on something that had never belonged to him.

Elliot and her parents didn't do much on Sundays. We went to church first thing that morning, and had brunch right after. We sat at a small table by the window inside the C&R Home-Style Café in downtown Lake Odessa. The café looked like a grandmother's dining room, but with extra sets of tables and chairs. I counted three chipped vases, and at least five different cat calendars. The atmosphere felt geriatric and stale. Ripped carpet and flowery tablecloths distracted me from the smiling faces of the employees.

I ordered half of a pot roast sandwich with a roll and mashed potatoes. I couldn't eat any of it. There was something blocking my brain, and I couldn't figure it out. Numbing myself to Warren and my uncle's hatred wasn't working as well as I would have liked. I didn't feel sad, but I felt sick—nauseous and anxious. What if my uncle never let me come home? What if I never saw my dad again? I didn't want to think about him, but I couldn't help it. If only he would come home and stand up to my uncle, put him in his place and kick him out into the streets. I hoped for it, but I knew it wouldn't happen. My dad would stay hidden.

At the Ways' that night, we all separated from one another. Elliot's dad worked out in the garage polishing his small pontoon boat for once the weather was nicer. Elliot stayed in her room talking on the phone, and Mrs. Way sat in the living room watching old black-and-white movies. She folded her family's laundry and hummed every song in every film. I sat with her because she seemed alone, even with her family being there. My family had never been this way. We all sat together always, and it had driven me crazy, but now I saw the point in it. We had been connected, and it felt nice to sit together in the

TV room watching Sunday night television while my mom cooked smothered pork chops and cream of mushroom rice. She had watched with us and laughed from the kitchen. It wasn't like that with the Ways. They were all disconnected.

The next morning at school, my neck felt stiff from sleeping on the couch again. Mrs. Way had re-washed my jeans the night before, and I was wearing one of Mr. Way's old t-shirts. It was too small for him, and it was too small for me. It made me even more self-conscious, and I was already dreading having to see Warren. I'd thought about it all through the night, and decided I needed to talk to Warren without Jared being there. I sat in homeroom behind Trish and next to Liza.

Liza talked for what felt like days about her performance.

"Did you see my assemblé at the end? It was perfect!" she squealed. "My mom missed the whole thing, but my teacher was so proud. She thinks I have real talent, and she wants to start a private lessons class with me on Saturday mornings."

"That's great, Liza," Trish said, hanging on her every word. "The way you moved, it was just—freaking amazing! You looked beautiful. I'm really proud of you too. I don't think I could ever have done anything so brave. Dancing in front of all those people? Girl, you rock."

Liza leaned back in her desk looking thoroughly pleased with herself, and that made me smile too. Her confidence had grown, just like Trish. They both seemed to finally notice that I was sitting there with them.

"Why are your clothes so wrinkled?" Liza asked me.

"Did your uncle try to do your laundry?" She let out a shrilling chuckle, proving that the Liza I had always known was still in there somewhere.

"I don't know what my uncle's doing," I said, exhaling. "I haven't seen him or Warren since Friday. He kicked me out the night of the fair."

"What night at the fair?" Liza asked. "Where have you been sleeping? I hope you haven't been sleeping out in the woods. You could have come and stayed with me," she argued.

"I'm not sleeping in the woods, more like camping out in Elliot's living room."

"But what about the fair?" Liza asked again.

"My dad took us to the fair when I got home on Friday," Trish blurted out. Her voice trembled whenever she lied. Liza would see straight through her. "It was a spur-of-the-moment type thing, and I knew you had dance rehearsal."

"But we always go to the fair together, the three of us. We've been going together every year since fifth grade. Why didn't you guys just wait until I could come along too?"

"I'm sorry, Liza," I said. I didn't want her to be upset with Trish because of me. "Look, it's my fault. I asked Trish to go, and she thought it would be weird without you, but I begged her to go anyway."

"Why did you want to go without me?" Liza asked without looking in my direction. My voice caught when she said that. There wasn't an answer I could give without hurting her feelings. She took my silence as a confirmation of her pitiful thoughts. "You two are going out now, aren't you?"

"No, definitely not," Trish said. "Why would you say that?"

"I don't believe you, Trish, so you can stop lying to me already!"

"Liza, it's not like that," I tried reasoning with her.

"Screw you, Stephen. You're such an inconsiderate jerk. You're both being terrible friends right now." Liza grabbed her books and walked out before the bell rang. I would have to fix this too. Trish and I stared at one another, not knowing what else could be said. Trish looked like she just had the wind knocked out of her. I opened my mouth to speak, and the bell rang at last. Trish grabbed her things and walked out, without looking at me—just as Liza had.

The pity wouldn't stop flowing the rest of the day, and Trish and Liza refused to speak to me. I felt like an idiot. How had I not predicted this would happen? I was coming between my two best friends. The most logical thing for them to do would be to forget about me. They both needed to exclude me from the friendship and carry on without me. That was the right thing to do, but I hoped they wouldn't do it. I needed them both. The night at the fair seemed like ages ago, and I couldn't help but wonder if Trish regretted the whole thing—even the kiss. The thought made me feel even worse. My stomach was in knots when I walked into the cafeteria. Trish and Liza sat at our usual table. Neither one looked at me when I walked up with my lunch tray. They weren't talking to me, but they weren't talking to each other either.

I pulled out the chair next to Liza, and she slammed it back into the table, again without looking at me. That was my cue, so I decided to sit alone for once. I found an empty spot at a long rectangular table near the cafeteria entrance and sat down. My stomach wouldn't stop flipping, and so I couldn't force myself to eat. But I wouldn't sit there and feel sorry for myself. Things weren't great, but they weren't desolate either. I could get through this. I would get through this. This was only a turning phase, a jumping off point of things to come. The loneliness didn't feel good, though, so I decided to go talk to Barry Patterson. I threw out my tray of uneaten food and headed for his basement office.

As I approached Barry's office, I noticed the lights were off and the door was shut. A hand-written note was taped on his door saying that he was out for the week due to a family emergency. This day couldn't get any worse. I wanted to feel lost and hopeless, but it wasn't time for that yet. The rest of the day went by without me noticing, even though I had hoped it would drag. I planned to wait until the last bell rang and then wait for Warren outside his locker. He'd be forced to talk to me.

Trish and I got the highest grade in our class for our science project on the moon and the tide. She still wasn't talking to me, but when we presented together, I caught her glancing at me. The class ended, and I rushed to leave so I could get to Warren's locker before he did. I saw him waiting at the bus stop that morning, so I knew he was in school today.

Trish walked over to my desk while I packed up my books. "I'm sorry," she breathed. "It wasn't right to blame you for Liza being pissed with me. She had every right to be pissed, and I should have told her the truth. I'm just not sure if it would do any good."

"What are you saying?" I asked her.

"Look, Stephen, I really like you, and I know you like me a lot too, but we need to just forget about the whole thing. This is going to kill our friendship with Liza, and with each other."

I nodded in understanding, but I couldn't say anything to her.

"Liza's said she'll walk home with us today. You up for it?"

"Yeah, sure," I said. My voice sounded distant and far-away. I tried to change my tone. "Look, I need to go. I want to talk to Warren. Can you guys wait for me?" Trish nodded.

Students crowded the halls, but as I stepped out of the classroom I saw that Warren wasn't at his locker yet. Most kids were grabbing their books or just hanging around talking and playing with one another. It was only Monday, but it felt like Friday. I stood there in the hall and waited for Warren, watching the other kids and trying to plan out my words.

When Warren walked up with Jared by his side, I noticed the cut under his left eye and the big dark circles around the top of his nose. Purple bruises covered his collarbone. I had to swallow back vomit from the sight. He smelled like home, and my uncle had already started in on him. I was still pissed with Warren, but he didn't deserve this.

"Did he do that?" I asked him. I needed him to listen if I had any chance of seeing my bedroom again.

Jared stood between us, blocking me from my own kid brother. "What the hell do you want?" he spat. I didn't bother to look at him.

"Why would it matter to you?" Warren said to me. "You left me with him, just like Dad. You're fucking useless." I could hear the anger burning him to the core.

"Can I talk to you alone?" I said to Warren, hoping he could hear my desperation. But then he stared at me like he wasn't seeing me. His eyes looked hazy, completely out of focus. He was high as a kite, in school. "What's wrong with you?" I asked, and he ignored me.

"Whatever you have to say to me you can say in front of Jared. Ready to come home, huh?" His expression was sadly smug. "No bitches allowed." He and Jared laughed. I leaned in to him so that Jared couldn't hear me, but he backed away. "Get the fuck away from me!" he said, and pushed me back.

"You miss Mom, Warren," I said. "You can stop acting like this because it's fine to miss her. I miss her too."

"I don't miss anybody. Not even you, so stay away from me."

"Look, you're pissed, and I get it. But stop taking out your anger on me. Stop comparing me to Dad. I'm not the one who left, and I'm all you've got right now."

"I don't need you. You don't understand shit," he said, puffing out his chest trying to look and sound tougher than he really was.

"It's okay to be mad about everything, Warren. She's dead. Mom's dead, and she's not coming back, and it isn't fair. So be mad about this, be mad all you want, but you can't stay bitter about this forever."

"I'm not angry," he breathed, and I saw his fists clenched at his sides. He wanted to hit me. I was going too far, but I couldn't stop the thoughts from pouring out of me.

"Yes, you are. You're mad as hell, and it has to stop. Stop skipping school. Stop drinking and smoking, and go back to hockey practice."

"Get out of here, asshole!" Jared shouted at me. He moved closer, standing inches away from my face. "He doesn't need you telling him how to feel." Jared punched me in the shoulder, but I didn't move.

"You miss her, Warren!" I shouted as Jared pushed me down the hall, further away from Warren. I stopped falling back and pushed Jared as hard as I could. He wrapped his arms around me, keeping me from getting to Warren. "Get off me! Don't fucking touch me, you piece of shit!" The familiar heat was building in my chest, and I tried to fight the aggression I was feeling. But Jared wouldn't stop fueling it. He wouldn't get off me. He wouldn't let go. And I couldn't get to Warren. I needed him to hear me. I struggled under Jared's weight as he tried to control my flailing arms.

"Talk to me, Warren!" I shouted. "Don't shut me out. I want to come home."

"Home? We don't have a home anymore. And there's nothing to talk about," Warren said, slamming his locker shut. He stood a few feet away from me with Jared in between. "I'm glad Mom's dead. Without her here, I can do whatever I want. I've never been happier."

That was the breaking point. "Warren doesn't need you," Jared said. "Give up, you stupid limping freak." He kneed me in my stomach. The heat took over. The halls of the school started to shake. Locker doors opened and shut. The big bulletin board by the entrance to the school fell to the ground. The windows in the hall shattered, and all the kids screamed and ran out of the school. Loose-leaf paper shot up toward the ceiling just as it had before, and everything swirled down the halls like a tornado. My mind whirred like an overheated laptop. I used my powers to push Jared and Warren down the hall. It was like watching the strength of the wind blow them away. Their bodies flew down the hall and crashed into a white, brick wall. Warren shouted out to me, but I couldn't hear a word he said. All I could hear was a ringing in my ears that grew louder as each ceiling light in the hall went out with a pop.

Mrs. Smith and a few of the administrators appeared at the other end of the hall. I didn't have time to make out their faces. They saw what I was doing. They knew it was me shaking the school's structure and causing the tornado of school supplies. Metal lockers dented, and their doors shot off into the hall. The chairs and tables in the cafeteria moved throughout the school, and I couldn't stop. The administrators rushed after me. I took off down the hall, but things were still happening all around me. Every window I ran by shattered, every light I ran under exploded. The floors and walls in the school started to crack, and the humming I always heard had turned into a screeching noise that forced everyone to cover their ears. It was me. I was doing all of it, and there wasn't anything I could do to control myself.

The principal called out my name and asked me to stay still.

"Stay where you are, Stephen," he said, trying to pacify me. "The police are on their way. We called your uncle, and everything's going to be okay. Just please stop doing whatever it is you are doing." The chaos continued. I stood still and turned to look at their faces. "Stop it right now!" he shouted, and I flung his body back and away from me, just as I'd done with Warren and Jared.

The principal fell back into the crowd of teachers and administrators, and I took off running. It was almost like I didn't have the limp, as my legs sprinted down the hall. I ran out of the school, and Trish and Liza stood at the bottom of the steps still waiting for me. They watched me in shock, calling out my name. I couldn't say anything. Some random kid left their bike unchained, so I hopped on it and pedaled as far away from the school as I could. I couldn't go back, not now, and not ever.

## CHAPTER 13

# A PLACE TO HIDE

MY HEART POUNDED as I pedaled down the streets that led to my house. This was bad. I didn't have anywhere to go, but I knew my uncle wasn't home yet. While he was out, I would grab all of my belongings and tow them away with me on the stolen bike.

Stephen the fugitive. Stephen the limping freak who almost blew up the school with his weirdness. Now more than ever before, I needed my dad. I needed an adult. For a moment as I slid my bike along frosted roads, I considered calling my dad and letting him know what had happened. I thought about screaming at him and demanding that he come home for my sake, and for Warren's. But I didn't. I wanted him to be the one to come to me. He was wrong for leaving us, and I couldn't let that go.

When I pulled up to my old brown house there were three police cars parked outside. The siren lights on their cars flashed. I counted seven cops total, including the one standing in the street talking to Mrs. Way. I hid behind Liza's purple-gray fence and tried to listen to what they were saying.

"You're out here waiting for Stephen Wilkes?" Mrs. Way asked in disbelief.

"Yep," the cop said, surveying the area with his arms folded across his chest. I could see the gold badge on the right side of his chest. "We've got at least 20 eyewitnesses claiming he's got some strange mind control power that he used to attack two kids and a principal."

"Do you realize how ridiculous this sounds?" she said. "I've known Stephen his whole life, and he doesn't have any telepathic powers. He's a normal kid whose mom just died. That boy is probably scared to death right now. And he's got nowhere to go."

"I hear you, but I'm just doing my job. I didn't see what happened. All I know is I'm supposed to wait here for the kid to show up. And when he does, we're arresting him."

"He's just a child. You can't arrest him."

My head was spinning. I had to get out of there before I ended up in a jail cell. My dad would have to come home if that happened. They were waiting to arrest me. All the cops in town were standing around waiting for the crazy kid. I was the crazy kid, so I took off in the opposite direction without a sound. Neither Mrs. Way nor the police officer turned to watch me ride off into the dusk. Luckily, they hadn't noticed me. The other cops were too busy looking for one kid to notice another. And so I took advantage and headed toward the east end of Lake Jordan. I wasn't sure what I expected to find, but I needed to calm down. My ears were still ringing, and I needed a bit of peace. No one would think to look for me out there.

Not a single soul walked along the edges of Lake Jordan. Very few people wandered over to the east end anyway. It wasn't as pretty, but that didn't matter to me. The stolen bike fell to the ground, and I walked to the edge of the water. I wasn't sure what I was expecting to see as I hovered over the water's surface, but I hoped my mom's face might stare back at me.

It didn't. She wasn't there. All I saw was my own olive-toned skin and dark blond hair. My eyes had shifted to a lighter shade of brown, though. I saw tiny flames around my irises, and they shined against the water's surface. The little light burning inside me needed to be extinguished. I wanted to be normal again. I didn't want to control things with my mind anymore. My eyes shut, tight, and I pictured the little light leaving my chest, but I still felt it there. I used my mind to collect some twigs and started a fire, deep in the trees. It helped to keep some of the chill at bay, but once the night began to stalk me, I had to put it out.

The sun sank lower into the distance. The barren trees of the east end embedded themselves on the backs of my eyelids. I lay on my back near the water's edge, staring up at the darkening sky. The tree branches formed an oddly shaped circle around the moon, encasing it. The branches seemed to hold a chunk of the sky in place. The moon peered down on me, bathing me in its dim light. I knew I would have to stay there until I could find a warmer place to hide. The night was frosty and bitter, and there was no shelter from the cold. A few flurries of snow fell, increasing my anxiety. The fire was dead. And so I slept there, freezing, as the sound of my chattering teeth echoed into the dead of night.

When I woke it was still dark, and my heart was beating out of my chest. It was trying to warn me. My eyes flew open. I knew that it was morning, but the sun hadn't woken up yet. Someone was calling my name. The sound was faint and falling, but I still heard it. Flashlights shined through the trees as several voices called out my name again. I heard two dogs barking. One leather shoe crunched down upon dead leaves. The town was searching for me. I stood up and stomped all over the branches where the fire had been the night before. If they found it, they'd know I'd been here. They kept calling out to me— in the voices of neighbors and friends, but they wanted to take me away from everything. I grabbed my jacket and mounted the bike.

My feet pedaled into the morning and led me to the outskirts of town. I needed a place to hide. I thought about going back to the clearing to search for answers and my own bike, but I didn't think I'd be able to find it again. They would expect me to go out to either Trish's or Liza's houses. I was sure my uncle had tipped the cops off as to who my friends were. There wasn't anyone who didn't already know I was a telepathic psycho out on the loose. Everyone knew what had happened at school. Everyone except for Barry Patterson who would be out all week. The sign that was taped to his door flashed through my vision. Barry lived just past the old fairgrounds. It seemed like ages ago when Elliot and I had passed his house along Hwy 52.

It wasn't safe, but riding along the highway was the only way I could think to find Barry's house again. People in town talked about Barry Patterson as if he was some kind of hoarder. I didn't know if it was true, but I'd seen firsthand the piles of junk he kept in his yard. Maybe his junk made him happy, and it definitely helped to distract your eyes from the awful, dried up maple trees that populated his yard.

Only two cars honked their horns at me as I trailed along slowly, searching for the guidance counselor's house. If I hadn't been paying such close attention, the house would have jumped out before me. It shocked me to see it, and my bike veered off into the freeway—another car horn blared. The house was another eyesore pasted on a dead-end road, surrounded by too much land, too much nothing. I steadied my handlebars and pulled off the highway and into Barry Patterson's front yard. His brown grass touched the tops of my knees, and his home was in desperate need of a paint job. At one time the house must have been a pale blue, but dirt and time had changed it to a brownish-gray. It was really early in the morning, and I guessed that Barry was still sleeping. I considered for a few seconds that there might be an actual emergency that was keeping him from school, but I didn't believe it.

The door to Barry's house was a faded bright red. Before knocking, I peered around the windows on the front porch. Barry sat in his pajamas and robe in front of his television, holding a bowl of cereal in his lap. He didn't look like he'd just experienced an emergency. There was beard stubble on his chin, and his face shined with grease. It looked like he hadn't showered in days. I tapped the glass of the window, and he jumped in his seat. He looked out the window and saw me standing there. I waved to him, and watched as he got up from the couch to open his front door.

"What are you doing here, Stephen?" Barry asked as he moved aside to let me in his house. "Students aren't supposed to visit me at my home."

"I know, but I really need to talk you," I said.

"We can talk in school." Barry assessed my tattered appearance. I guessed I looked just like I felt, as if I'd slept in the woods unintentionally for the second time this year. "Is this about one of the things you don't want to talk about?"

"Yes," I said. "But I'm still not sure if I should talk about this or not. Something bad happened at school yesterday. Why weren't you there?"

"I had some personal things I needed to take care of. What happened?" he asked, holding the door open for me. Barry moved into the living room, and I followed him inside.

"What kind of personal things?" I asked.

"Personal enough that I don't feel like you need to know."

"That's great," I said, and Barry asked me why. "Because I can't tell you what happened at school, and you don't really need to know," I said. "You keep your secret, and I'll keep mine, deal?" Barry Patterson eyed me with suspicion as I walked around his living room. I couldn't tell him the truth. He wouldn't believe me. "Can I stay here with you, Mr. Patterson?"

"Don't you think you should go home to your uncle

and brother?" he asked. "I'm sure they're both worried about where you are."

"They're not worried at all, and if I go home the cops will just arrest me." I plopped down on Barry's couch and reached for the television remote. He was watching court TV, and I hated court TV. I switched the station to cartoons and adjusted myself for comfort, propping my feet up on his coffee table. Barry's house felt like home to me.

"Stephen, you need to tell me what happened at school."

"You first," I said, staring at the television screen. His features turned up in question. "Tell me your secret first, and then maybe I'll tell mine."

"I had to go to court yesterday," Barry said. "My wife and I are finalizing our divorce this week. Now will you tell me what happened, or do I need to call the school?"

"You're getting a divorce, why?" I asked. Why had I trusted anything he said about how marriages worked? He couldn't even hold his own together.

"That's beside the point."

"I listened to you," I said. "I thought you knew what you were talking about, but I guess it was all just bullshit, huh?"

Barry stood in front of me, blocking my view of the television.

"Look, sometimes things don't work out with the person you choose. That's just life; it's no one's fault. I wasn't well enough to take care of my wife, and so she left me. I know what it's like to feel the way you're feeling, to have hopelessness holding on to your tongue with an iron grip. You want to say something, but you feel like it's too late. I know what that's like, and I meant everything I said during our visits. But that doesn't change the fact that you shouldn't be here, Stephen."

I lowered my voice. "I don't have anywhere else to go, Mr. Patterson. No one can know that I'm here. You're all I have right now. Do you get that?" I said, unable to look at him. It was weird seeing him like this. He looked like a real person and not just the eccentric guidance counselor. The robe didn't suit him. I wanted him to put on his khakis and a button-up shirt.

"You need to tell me what happened, Stephen. I could lose my job over this, and my house, considering my divorce has left me bankrupt."

He looked pitiful standing there in his dingy old robe, so I explained everything that had been going on, except the part about my feelings. I left out all the talk about real feelings and just talked about the levitation stuff. He seemed to understand what had gone on in school.

"You caused all of this, you're sure?" he asked me as he sat at a tiny old table that had been pushed into a corner. He sipped on a cup of coffee, which I watched him get up to refill three times. I guessed all adults had some form of addiction. "And they saw you do it?"

I nodded. "When I went home after school yesterday, there were a ton of cop cars waiting out there for me. They're hunting me down. What am I supposed to do?"

"Stay here," he said. "For right now, the best thing to do is stay here. You're just a kid, and no one was hurt. But you shouldn't tell anyone else what you told me. They have to prove you did this without a doubt, and if what you've just told me is true, then I see no way for them to prove this. I mean, this all sounds like magic, and I don't believe in magic." He paused. "Can you show me how you're able to move objects?"

My instinct was to show him without a second thought. But something stopped me cold, and I thought better of it. Even though I trusted Barry, I didn't need any more witnesses. "I can only do it when I'm upset," I said. "I don't have any control over it." I felt bad for lying to him, because he'd taken me into his home, but I didn't have a choice.

"It's alright," he told me. "Everything's going to be fine. I'm going to hop in the shower, and when I get out we'll figure out what to do next. Just sit here and watch cartoons. There's food in the fridge if you're hungry." Barry walked off toward his bedroom. Alarms sounded in my head. Something didn't feel right, but I wanted to trust Barry Patterson, so I ignored my instincts. I heard the shower running. The water made a gushing sound in the walls as it traveled down rusty pipes. A loud clanging noise made me jump to my feet, and I walked down the hall to find out what had caused the sound. Once, my mom fell in the shower when no one was home, so I felt the need to check on Barry.

The door to Barry's bedroom was shut, and I pressed my ear to the wood to hear what he was doing. I heard muffled voices, whispered tones over the sound of the water rushing.

"Yes, that's what I said. He's at my home off Hwy 52. I didn't want to call his uncle, but I'm worried about him. He just showed up here, and he really believes he caused whatever happened to the school. I think his grief has gotten to him and…" I listened as Barry trailed off. "You're not serious—you're saying everyone believes he did it? That's not possible. People don't use their minds to move objects." I could hear him sighing into the phone. "No, he doesn't know I've contacted the police. Just get here. I don't know what to do with him."

I listened as Barry hung up the phone and walked toward the door. The shower water was still running in the background. My heart started to beat too fast again. My chest tightened, and I could feel the heat building. Barry flung open the bedroom door and stared at me. My limbs were shaking, and I could hear the floorboards cracking.

"What's happening?" Barry asked when the house swayed as if it were crumbling. "Are you okay, Stephen?" I backed away from him, keeping my eyes fixed on his as I moved down the hall. "Where are you going?" he asked, and I didn't stop backing away from him. "You need to stay here, Stephen." He held up his hands in surrender, but he didn't move toward me. "This isn't your fault. We're going to get you the help you need."

I was still fizzing over like a pop that had sat in the sunlight for too long. Barry's hands grabbed for me, and I jumped back. We backed each other in to his living room, and he looked up at all of the objects in his home—the coffee table, magazines, books, glasses and plates, all floating in midair, spinning and turning, bouncing off the walls. Barry lunged at me, and a lamp struck him on the head. He fell over onto the ground, and I ran. I ran right out the front door and back down the highway.

# CHAPTER 14

# THE SEARCH BEGINS

MY MIND CLOUDED over as I made my way through the trees. I was determined to stay hidden, so I walked a mile off from the main highway. My instincts fell flat as fear struck me. The brushes covered my lanky figure as I walked along, cold and weary. It was still light out, but I had no clue what time it was. I couldn't see my shadow so I guessed it was early in the afternoon. I worried about Barry. He might be hurt, lying there on the floor unconscious. I felt guilty, but he'd ratted me out. The police were probably there by now anyway. They wouldn't let him die. It was strange that I'd trusted him so much before, and now he just seemed sad. I felt bad for Barry Patterson. I felt worse for him than I did for myself because I still had time to fix things. His time was running out, and he didn't have anyone in his life to take care of him.

The day dragged on as I tried to think of a plan. The darkness chased me, and I stopped to rest every now and then. The last time I'd wandered through these woods, I worried about getting lost. I wasn't afraid to get lost now; in fact, it was my goal. If I lost myself, then no one else would be able to find me. It was more than logical to me, and so I wandered through the forest without any sense of direction. Shadows emerged, shapes of blackness that followed me everywhere. I couldn't fight the time. My gut churned as paranoia set in. It felt like someone really was following me, watching my every move. A branch snapped in the distance. I could hear two sets of tiny footsteps nearby. But the footsteps were before me, not behind me.

"Stephen," a familiar voice called out to me. It almost sounded like my mom. I followed the voice hoping it would lead me back to the clearing just as the little light had. Two small frames moved behind the trees. I froze in place, worried it might be another search party. But where were the flashing lights and barking dogs? Someone embraced me from behind. The arms were thin and warm, far too familiar. I stared down at the skin. It was pale and daunting. I smiled as Liza gripped my forearms. I turned around to face her, and saw Trish by her side.

"We didn't think we'd ever see you again," Trish said, and they both hugged me. The pain I felt began to fade. There were people who still cared about me. I wasn't completely alone.

"How did you find me?" I asked. We were standing in a circle so we could see each other's faces. The position reminded me of when we were in elementary school and used to huddle together on the blacktop to fight the freezing air.

"It wasn't easy," Liza said. "This morning, I saw the

cops outside your house waiting for you, so I knew you hadn't gone home last night. Elliot's mom was screaming in the street that they needed to lock up your uncle, and I decided to ask Elliot if she knew where you were."

"Elliot wouldn't have known," I told them.

"Well, she didn't know where you were, but I thought to ask her about a few weeks ago, when she found you along the highway. She said you were all the way out by Mr. Patterson's house. So I figured if we walked through the woods we'd find you eventually." Liza looked more than satisfied with her detective skills.

"And your parents know you went looking for me?" I asked.

They both looked like I'd just caught them walking into the boy's bathroom. "We sort of ran away," Trish said, looking only at Liza. I stayed quiet and waited for an explanation. "We left notes for them, so we weren't heartless about it or anything. We just wanted them to worry about us. You know what I mean, Stephen."

"No, I don't know what you mean."

"Look, Stephen, we knew you wouldn't be able to go home ever again, and our parents... well, our parents suck. They ignore us, and school's awful, so we decided to meet up with you and live in the woods," Liza said. "There can't be anything worse than living our miserable lives. We're craving the adventurous life."

"Have you both forgotten just how good you have it?" I asked. They watched me as I rocked back on my heels in frustration. "You're both going home right now. This is my problem. I'm the one who's been exiled, and you're not going to suffer because of my freak-like abilities."

"But this is textbook small-town drama," Liza whined. "There's no way you're getting all the glory. We want to do something daring, and I wish you would try to get rid of us, Stephen Wilkes! Just go ahead and try. See what happens. I dare you, fool," Liza taunted me.

"You two can stay for now, but you're going back to school tomorrow."

"School's out next week anyway. It's Thanksgiving, remember?"

What did Thanksgiving matter when you didn't have a family? I didn't say that to them, but I felt it. Things weren't perfect in either of their lives, but they still had it better than me. They weren't wanted by the town. And they still had their families. They still had their moms.

"So what's the plan?" Trish asked me.

"I don't have one," I admitted.

"Well, we need one," Trish decided. "We're going to have to figure out a way to change you back to the way you were before. The town's going to persecute you if we don't."

"I already tried," I told them. "Nothing's worked." They didn't need to know that I had only tried once, and it hadn't been a solid attempt.

"But you said everything changed the night you found that light in the clearing, right?" Trish wasn't looking for a response. She was only thinking aloud. "That means we need to get back to the clearing. If we can find it again, then maybe we can change you back."

"But how's that going to fix anything?" Liza asked.

"Well, this whole thing is going to trial, don't you think?" Liza and I shrugged. "It will, trust me, it will,"

Trish reasoned. "Our town's crooked, but it's not slanted. They wouldn't do that, they'd give you a fair trial, and if you're not able to do these strange things anymore, then they don't have any proof."

"They've got eyewitnesses," I told her.

"Eyewitnesses who saw what?" Trish said. "All they saw was a bunch of random occurrences that they can't pin on you. Their case is weaker than applesauce."

Liza and I groaned at her bad joke.

"But why do we have to change him back?" Liza groaned. "He's much more interesting this way." I stuck my tongue out at her. "Why can't Stephen just pretend that he can't do the floating stuff anymore?"

"He can pretend all he wants, but they're going to try and provoke him. I'm sure your uncle's already told the police about the night you tossed the kitchen table at him."

Liza chimed in. "Yeah, and you know Warren's blabbed about the incident in the hall a few weeks ago."

"You really think Warren would sell me out like that?"

Neither of them knew what to say. A part of me wanted to believe that Warren was still good. He wouldn't rat me out. Warren still loved me. He was the only hope I had left besides the two people standing next to me. No one said another word, and so we built a fire and decided to search for the clearing the next day. Trish and Liza collected branches for the fire, and I started it with thoughts of heat. Trish had thought to bring sleeping bags, bottles of water, food, and a tiny flashlight packed in an enormous backpack that her dad used for hunting. We took turns keeping watch for wild animals, and I kept the fire burning. It didn't feel like we were hiding from the world. It felt like we were camping out on an adventure, just as Liza said.

Dawn broke through the trees. I hadn't slept the entire night, and I watched my two best friends as the sunlight stirred them awake. Trish sat up in her sleeping bag to stretch and yawn. She caught me staring, and turned the other way. Liza opened one eye, then the other, and rolled back over, pretending to sleep.

"No," she whined. "It can't be morning already. I'm not ready to wake up."

"Just get up," Trish said, rolling up her sleeping bag. "We've got a long day of searching ahead of us."

"Do you guys know if they're still looking for me?" I asked. "I'm worried they might find us before we can find the clearing."

They both looked at each other. "Let's just try to find the clearing as quickly as possible," Trish said. "If we go about this the right way it should only take a day, right?"

"Yeah, and then what?" I asked. My optimism was fading. I wasn't sure if everything was going to be okay. Life had a way of working itself out. I believed that, I really did, but I also felt that this fell outside the realm of normal trials and tribulations.

"Then we go back to your house." Trish was packing up as she spoke, and she stopped short, staring off into the distance. "Let's call your dad," she said. "He needs to know what's going on right now."

"If my dad cared, he'd be home right now. If my dad cared, none of this would have happened," I said, feeling completely out of control, but still managing to maintain a calmness within my tone. "My uncle wouldn't be in our house, and Warren wouldn't be starting so much trouble. My dad is the reason for everything, and he's not even worried if his sons are dead or alive."

"He might be so sad right now that he can only take care of himself," Trish said. "You don't know what he's going through."

"And he doesn't know what I'm going through. He doesn't care, Trish, can't you see that? Why is everyone defending him? This is wrong. Leaving us with my shitty uncle was wrong."

I sat on the ground next to where the fire had burned. Liza walked over to me and put her hand on my shoulder. She didn't say anything, but when I looked into her eyes it felt like I could read her mind. Liza agreed with every word I said, but she still felt bad for my dad. There was still pity for him in her eyes, and I didn't know how to feel about that.

"Where's your mom's cell phone?" Trish asked.

"It's at home in my sock drawer," I said, but I couldn't help feeling my pants pocket to see if it was there. I ran my fingers along the stitching, and there it was, but I didn't remember putting the cell phone there when I left my house the day of the fair. "No, wait," I said, turning to face them both. "Here it is. It was in my pocket. I must have forgotten I put it there." Before the words came out, I felt like I was playing a game. Nothing seemed real anymore.

"Have you checked it lately?" Trish asked, and I shook my head. "I can't believe it still has half the battery life. That's insane."

"I charge it every once and a while," I admitted. It was weird, and it didn't make sense. If I was so pissed at my dad, then there was absolutely no reason for me to keep reading his desperate text messages to my dead mom. I watched Trish as she scrolled through a few of the most recent. She turned the phone off and put it in her knapsack, without looking back at me. I saw her do it, but I didn't say anything about it. Let her keep it if that's what she wanted.

We spent half the morning retracing my steps from the night I went searching for Warren. They didn't understand why I couldn't remember what street I was on when I found the forest. It didn't make sense to me either, but that was the only reason I could give them. As we searched, Liza complained about her legs hurting. She complained about it being too cold and about being hungry. She complained that her pants were too tight and her wool coat was too snug. After a time, I was able to tune her out, but Trish refused to.

"If you complain about one more thing," Trish shouted at Liza, "I'm going to rip out your voice box so I don't have to hear your whining. You sound like a toddler."

"I'm not complaining," Liza whined. "I'm just trying to make conversation. No one else is saying anything."

The sound of their arguing voices faded into the background. At some point they'd stopped walking to scream at each other, and I kept on. I turned back to look at them and saw they hadn't noticed I was no longer standing beside them. I was glad they were here, but I couldn't stop worrying about what Trish said in science class a few days ago. Things were still awkward between us. Whenever she caught me staring she shook her head at me, as if that helped in any way. I wouldn't ever be able to stop staring at Trish. It hurt that she didn't want to try with me. She didn't think it was worth jeopardizing our friendship over, and maybe that was true. But I didn't want to believe it. My thoughts about her weren't going to change any time soon. Especially, since the majority of my time was spent with her and Liza. Things couldn't go back to the way they were before; it didn't feel the way it had always felt.

"Stephen agrees with me," I heard Liza say. I kept walking. "Stephen, come back!"

"You guys are wasting time," I told them. "Getting irritated with each other isn't going to change the situation."

"I'm sorry, Trish," Liza said. "I didn't realize I was complaining. I'll try to stop."

"It's okay," Trish said. "We're all on the edge right now. Let's keep looking. You said you left your bike near the freeway, Stephen?"

The way she said my name sounded better than keeping time. I smiled, but I didn't let her see it. She would have just shaken her head at me. Her frosty attitude was getting to me. It was as if she hadn't kissed me, and I knew it had been real—the whole thing. Trish could try to deny the way she felt about me all she wanted. I knew her crush was still there.

"Isn't this your bike?" Liza asked. I turned around and saw my silver, three-speed bicycle lying in a pile of dead leaves. Trish inspected its positioning.

"He must have come from Abbots Road, then." Trish wouldn't look at me. It was as if she knew exactly what I was thinking. I watched her mock the way I held on to my handlebars, and then she picked the bike up and sat down. She did this twice more before turning to Liza, "Yep, he definitely came into the forest down this way."

"Aren't you going to ask me?" I said. "And I have a name, you know. You don't have to sit there and pretend like I don't exist. Looking in my direction isn't going to kill you."

"What way did you come into the forest, Stephen?" She emphasized each syllable of my name. I was pissing her off, but I didn't care.

"The clearing's this way." I decided to let it go. There were more important things to worry about than whether Trish still had her crush. Although it was taking up far too much space in my brain. I didn't look back at them as I led the way, but I saw the empty space between the trees. The patch of earth stretched out before me, and I stepped out into the open. The space lit a flame inside me. It was too much seeing it again. My limbs locked in place, and Trish and Liza walked up on either side of me.

CHAPTER 15

# THE CHANGING PLACE

"THIS PLACE IS really creepy," Liza said, staring at the dozens of dead trees. "What made you walk out into this clearing? The animals won't even come out here." Two dark brown squirrels ran along the perimeter of dying trees. The clearing felt different in the light of day. There was an eeriness to it. A lonely sound echoed through these barren trees. Our shallow breathing and our shoes crunching down on fallen branches was all we could hear. We stayed still and silent, our eyes drifting from left to right.

"Where were you when you saw the light?" Trish asked.

I walked them over to the place where I remembered the light dancing. We stared at it, hoping something might happen. And when nothing happened, I decided to lead them to the pond. This was the part I was dreading, the part I would have liked to be alone for. I had never told them about seeing my mom's reflection. I had never told them about the letter I found. It would be different now if I looked in the water and saw her face staring back at me. I would be seeing her face with new eyes, eyes that knew she'd jeopardized our happiness for her own self-ish reasons. Everyone was selfish, I decided as I looked at Trish. She didn't care about my feelings at all. I'd given her the chance to choose, but she hadn't given it to me.

They watched as I walked up to the pond and leaned in. I looked down, and again my mom's reflection wasn't there. Nothing but my own face stared back at me. I couldn't recapture the way I'd felt that night. I thought back and remembered feeling hopeless, trapped by my uncle and all my new responsibilities. I had been worried about Warren, if I'd ever see him again, because I knew I wouldn't ever see my mom again.

That was the night everything hit me. The loss of my mom had finally set in when I read those texts from my dad. Before that night, I was going about life and everything else as if I were already dead. My thoughts and feelings locked deep inside me. That was the night I found the cell phone, and the night I lost the numbness. It had occurred to me several times that I'd imagined seeing her that night. It also occurred to me that maybe she'd been reaching out to me, letting me know she still loved me and that everything was going to be fine. The second one was the one I wanted to believe, but I didn't.

I saw a water droplet ripple in the pond. It wasn't raining. I touched my face and felt tears there. I rubbed them away with the sleeve of my jacket so Trish and Liza wouldn't see. The last thing I needed was the two of them knowing that I cried. I wasn't sure why it mattered; it's not like either of them saw me as tough. I just wanted them to think I was stronger, more resilient than to cry over not seeing a hallucination again.

"There's nothing here," I said as they stood behind me and the pond. The evening had set in. Shadows roamed the clearing. Omens sounded through the dusk. "This was a waste of time. We came here for nothing. I'm just going to turn myself in."

"If you turn yourself in, they will definitely call your dad. It's not like your uncle has any guardianship of you or Warren. We need your dad here to resolve this, Stephen."

"Okay, Trish," I said. "Since you seem to have an answer for everything, tell me what to do. You don't care about what I think, so you go right ahead and call all the shots, boss."

She rolled her eyes, but still wouldn't look at me. She wanted to say something smart. The urge was eating away at her, but she held her tongue. "Let's call your dad, please?" Her tone was sweet. It didn't match the tension in her high cheekbones.

"You're fake, Trish," I blurted out. It was completely true, but also completely unfair. "You won't look at me. Everything you've said to me has been frosty, and you know it."

"Stop it. Now's not the time," she whispered. She knew exactly what I was referring to. "We need to call your dad. He *will* help us. Don't you want him to come home?" She was making a conscious effort not to look at the knapsack resting on her hip.

"If he wanted to come home, he would have. Give me the phone," I snapped, reaching for her knapsack.

"I don't have it," she lied right to my face. I couldn't hide my disappointment. "Fine, I have it, but I'm not giving it back to you until you listen to what I have to say."

"Give me the damn phone. He's my dad, not yours, and I can make my own decisions."

"Stephen," Liza chimed in. "She's just trying to help. What were you hoping to find here? It's obvious you're holding something back. Just tell us what you're thinking. We wouldn't judge you, and we know you've been having a tough time. Anyone would be a little bit fragile right now."

"Everything's a mess," I muttered and sat down on the ground. "I'm scared. I'm really fucking scared right now." My hands were shaking, but I didn't cry in front of them. I wouldn't. "I don't know what's happening to me, and I just thought… I just thought that maybe I'd be able to see her face again. I don't know. That sounds crazy, but when everything changed, here, that night, I saw my mom's face in that pond, and now I can't remember what she looks like. What if I can't ever remember?"

Liza moved first and sat down on the ground next to me. She rested her head on my shoulder. Trish wanted to comfort me too; I could see in her eyes just how torn she felt, reaching for something she couldn't grasp. I wanted to hold on to it too, but she wouldn't let me. I felt even more rejection as she turned away from us.

"You won't ever forget her, okay?" Liza said. "She's here. I know it. I miss her too," she breathed. "You weren't the only person to lose her, Stephen. And you can talk about it. It's okay if you talk in circles; just let it out. If you don't, it's going to kill you."

"There are times when I can't stop replaying the way things used to be," I whispered. "And sleeping in that house night after night," I groaned in exasperation, "I just can't. I can't anymore. I don't know if I'll ever be able to go back there. It's like torture, but it's the only place where I can feel her, so I don't want to let it go. I thought I felt her here, but there's nothing now," I said, keeping my voice even.

"Don't you think your dad feels that way?" Trish said.

"What way?" I asked.

She sucked in air and walked further away from Liza and me. "You just said it's like torture being in that house, and you only loved your mom, you weren't *in* love with her like your dad. Can't you imagine that being in that house, where he'd spend every day with her, might be hard for him too?"

I hadn't thought about that, and I wasn't ready to resolve my feelings about my dad. It was obvious he was depressed, heartbroken, and so desperate that he was reaching out to someone he wouldn't ever hear from again. He was delusional.

"Don't you get it?" Trish asked.

"He has responsibilities, Trish. You can't let everything go just because you get sad, and I know because I've had to do everything while he's been away. I've had to put up with my inebriated, shitty-ass uncle because of him. That's what's real," I said. "That night when I saw my mom was the toughest thing for me because my dad wasn't there. My uncle threw me out into the cold to find my own kid brother. I'd never felt so alone and insane. I saw her face that night, and that's when the light jumped inside me. Once I tried to touch her reflection, it faded away." I paused to look at them. "Am I losing it?"

"No, I don't think so," Liza said, leaning in to me and picking at her cuticles. "You're not crazy. You did see her, Stephen. You were meant to, I think. I mean, doesn't it seem strange that you just happened to find this clearing that night, and that you just happened to see your mom's reflection? I just don't think it was a coincidence."

"But I can't feel her here anymore," I said, frustrated that they weren't asking the right questions. It wouldn't be possible for me to just share what I'd read in the letter—they'd have to pry it out of my mind and view it on a computer screen.

"Let's wait until nightfall," Trish said, moving back toward us. She didn't sit down, but at least she was looking at me. "Maybe it has to be dark." She shrugged with uncertainty.

"I'm afraid to see her again," I said. "I'm worried she might not look the same."

"What's changed since that night?" Trish asked, staring down at Liza and me.

I wasn't sure how to talk about this, and I didn't know why it felt embarrassing for me to say out loud. Maybe I felt like my parents' bad decisions were somehow a reflection of me. "My mom, she cheated on my dad before she died." I paused and let it all out, "When I went through their stuff that day, I found this letter in an old box of photos, and it was... it was the saddest thing I've ever read. And it changed my memories about her."

"What did it say?" Liza asked. "Are you sure your

mom was being serious? Maybe she was just playing some kind of joke."

"It wasn't a joke," I said. "This was real. She said all this stuff about hating herself and that my dad knew what *he did*. She said she was going crazy and that's why she did it."

"Who's he?" Liza asked.

"I don't know," I said. "But my dad knows, and that's what I want to find out. Whatever *he did*, that's what made her go crazy."

"And your dad forgave her?" Trish asked. "Just like that, he acted like nothing had ever happened? I can't believe that. It doesn't make sense." She was crying, and I didn't think it would be okay for me to touch her, even though that was all I wanted to do. I asked her what was wrong. I sat up on the ground and moved toward her.

She backed away. "It's nothing," she said, wiping at her eyes. "It's just my mom thinks… well she doesn't know, but she thinks my dad is having an affair. That sounds silly, right? I mean, he loves us." It sounded like she was asking us if we thought it might be true. I couldn't say anything that wouldn't lead to more hurt, so I stayed quiet and kept my distance. "I texted your dad back," she admitted to me. "I'm sorry. I just felt so bad for him, and now I feel even worse for him. I don't regret it."

"How could you do that, Trish?" Liza asked. "It's only going to make it worse for him. What did you text him?"

"I just said 'I'm sorry.' That was all I typed, and then I hit send. That's all, Stephen, I swear. It was supposed to make him feel better. He misses her. She was his wife."

"You think you know what's best for everyone!" I was

screaming. "But you don't know what's best for me or my dad, Trish. You're some fourteen-year-old girl with a high I.Q. You might be smart, but you don't know anything about people. You should have let me decide for myself, instead of just taking over."

"I was just helping, that's all. It's not going to change anything, but it might give him a little bit of hope, and then he'll be able to come home, and everything will go back to the way it was before."

"Things will never go back to the way they were. It doesn't work like that, Trish." I paced back and forth across the clearing, waving my arms around like a mad-man. "They just can't!"

"Yes, they can," Trish cried. "Things can always go back. You don't know shit!" She was full-on balling, and I wasn't sure if it was just about her parents, or if some of it had to do with me. Liza walked toward Trish and embraced her. She let Trish cry into her shoulder, and I wanted it to be me. Even though I was so mad at Trish I could have set fire to the ground, I wanted to be there for her. I was just too stubborn to admit it. Trish sniffled, and her crying stopped. "Why are you so determined to give up?" she asked.

"I'm not giving up," I said. "I just know that it doesn't work like that, Trish. You can't go back, only forward."

We stayed in the clearing until nightfall, just as Trish had suggested. There wasn't any other resolution to reach, as we were all so raw from sitting with our thoughts. Trish drifted off to sleep, gripping her jean knapsack. All the crying must have tired her out, because she wasn't the type who slept soundly in the woods. I wasn't that type either, and so I couldn't sleep. The cold, hard ground dug into my bones. Liza was still awake, but we weren't speaking to each other, just staring off into the distance, listening for danger. No one ever tells you just how frightening it is to be outside, at night, or how every sound makes you jump, how the night plays tricks on your eyes. I wasn't alone, but I felt alone.

I wondered if Trish was dreaming about me as I watched her chest rise and fall. Did she ever see my face in her mind as she slept? I laughed. If she was thinking about me, it was just about how much she hated me. Things wouldn't ever be the same again. We were all growing up, and I didn't know if I could just stay friends with Trish. We'd be in high school next year, and I couldn't take watching her go out with other guys. And then having to hear all the details, like I was just her friend. It would kill me if she put me back in the same category as Liza, especially since I knew she liked me too. She did like me, but she wanted to forget. My chest ached. Maybe I was something to forget?

Liza eventually fell asleep too. She'd hung on for my sake, but gave in to her weary eyes. The life drained out of me as my thoughts sank further and further into the abyss. My mom had left me here all alone to stand up to her brother, to protect myself against him. This wasn't the way it was supposed to work. I wasn't supposed to worry about keeping myself safe; that was a parent's job, but I didn't have any parents left.

Loneliness pecked at my eyes, making it too difficult for me to close them. And then I heard my mom's voice humming in my head. The sound was soft and quiet as it carried through the dark forest. I couldn't place the tune, but it felt like home. It was as if I were sitting at the kitchen table while she made chocolate chip cookies. She'd always hummed when she baked, and I could hear it now. It was distant, almost like a faint ringing in my ears, but it was her. I knew it. And I knew what was meant to happen next.

I walked away from my slumbering best friends and toward the pond once again. My body knew something was about to happen as my heart fluttered in my chest. It skipped—I mean it really skipped, and I let out a gasp. And there she was. Her sad, smiling face reflected upon the water. She looked like she was laughing as the night wind moved the water. I couldn't smile back at her, though. I was too desperate to know why she hurt my dad, and why she hated herself. Happy moms don't hate themselves, and her positivity had always been my light. I thought someone had stolen my light since then, and I couldn't see through the darkness.

She frowned as I watched her with my new eyes. I saw her guilt staring back at me. I saw her pain and all her hurt, but what had caused it? I wanted to ask her. I needed her to hear me, but there wasn't any hope for that. I leaned over the pond, pleading with my eyes, and her reflection mouthed the word "home." I wanted to cry for her grief and my own. She wanted to come home, and I wanted nothing more than to speak to her again. I reached out my hand to touch her, and her reflection faded as my own mirrored its position. I saw myself in the water, and the light burning in my chest. It looked like it had separated from my body, but it hadn't. I could still feel it there. My heart skipped again. I let out another gasp and fell to the ground. The little light was stealing my air. It was stealing my sense of self. I couldn't move, I felt so heavy from the weight of my worries, the weight of the light. But somehow I drifted off to sleep. And for the first time since her death, I dreamed about my mom.

# CHAPTER 16

# ONLY IN MY DREAMS

"**Y**OU'RE GOING TO be late if you don't get out of bed this instant!" My mom screamed at me from her bathroom. Her voice wasn't difficult to place in our small home. "Stephen Wilkes! Get out here right now!" she called.

The light shined in through the cracks of the broken blinds in my bedroom. My room was the biggest in the house, and that wasn't saying much. It was even bigger than my parents', although I didn't have a bathroom. My twin bed was pushed into the far left corner, right next to the only window. It was a large window off the back of the house, and you could see the lake through the tress from the view. The light from the window forced my eyes open. My dad had painted my bedroom walls an off-white color, but they looked blue in the early mornings. The smell of too-crisp bacon and French toast wafted through the halls.

There was a knock on my bedroom door. "Stephen, you decent?" my dad asked. I didn't respond, but he walked in *anyway, shutting the door behind him. I hopped out of bed and pulled on my jeans from a pile of clothes on the floor. "Your floor isn't a clothes hamper, kid." He laughed and pulled me close. I didn't hug him back, but he didn't seem to care. "Your mom's going to kill you if you don't get out of here. Get to bed late?"*

*"Sort of," I muttered, pulling off my shirt from the day before. I searched through the drawers of my dresser for a clean one. The pile on the floor smelled like stale body odor. "Just started re-reading some H.G. Wells and lost track of the time," I said.*

*"Better the second time?" he asked, and I shrugged. "Can we talk for a minute?"*

*"Not now, Dad," I said. "I'm running late, and I need to eat some breakfast." I threw a striped navy-blue shirt over my head and raced down the hall. My dad followed me to the kitchen. He grabbed his coffee and watched me stuff six pieces of burnt bacon into my mouth.*

*"Well, don't worry about chewing," he laughed. "Let's go. I'll drive you, that way you won't be late. And we can talk for a bit."*

*"Where's Warren," I muttered, chewing on a piece of French toast. My mom put so much powdered sugar on it that it didn't need syrup.*

*"He's already at the bus stop. He got up the first time your mom called."*

*"Sorry," I said, my mouth still stuffed with food. I grabbed a glass of orange juice and gulped it down.*

*"Is Stephen awake yet?" my mom asked from the hall.*

*"We're in the kitchen, sweets," my dad called out to her. She walked up to him as he leaned against the kitchen coun-*

*ter. My mom put her arms around his neck, and he embraced her waist. They kissed, and I let out a groan.*

*"Can't you two do that when I'm sleeping?" I said and grabbed my backpack from the coat closet next to the front door.*

*My mom poured herself a cup of coffee and sat down at our decaying kitchen table. She spoke to me from the kitchen. "Did you get all your homework done?" she asked while I searched through my bag, making sure I had everything I needed.*

*"Sort of," I muttered. The book had grabbed me and pulled me in last night. It had taken me hostage, and I couldn't put it down, so my eyes had made the decision for me. Most of my homework was done except for a few math problems I was hoping to finish in homeroom.*

*"He got too busy reading another one of his sci-fi books," my dad added his two cents. "Reading is much more important than schoolwork," he said sarcastically.*

*"Dad!" I shouted. "We need to leave right now. I don't want to be late!"*

*"Alright, kiddo," my dad said. "Give me a sec to say good-bye to your mom."*

*"You'll see her again tonight," I complained. "It's only a few hours."*

*"You're driving him, then?" my mom asked, and my dad confirmed. "Well, great, Stuart, now I'm going to have to pick him up on my way home from the store."*

*"Make him take the bus. Warren takes the bus."*

*"He can't take the bus," my mom said. "That Jared kid is going to give him trouble. And I refuse to see him battered and blue ever again."*

"It was one time," I groaned. "You don't have to keep bringing it up. Dad!"

"Kasey called last night," my dad said. "I told him you were asleep and would call him today. He sounded pretty off. You might want to call him back."

Sadness touched the corners of my mom's eyes. "Not today," she said, stifling something that sounded caught in her throat. "I just can't take having to hear his voice today."

"Don't worry about it," my dad said. "Let your mom deal with him."

"Dad, please," I said, gripping the door handle.

"Alright," my mom said. "You two get out of here. Come give your mom a kiss. You can't just walk out of here without telling me bye." I walked up to her in slow-paced defiance as she sat at the kitchen table. She pulled me close, and I kissed her quickly on the cheek. It wasn't that I didn't love my mom, but I didn't like to be babied. And kissing her good-bye made me feel like the biggest kid ever. "I love you, my sweet boy." She crooned. "But God loves you more."

My dad and I hopped into the cab of his old green pick-up truck. The doors were heavy, old, and they squeaked whenever someone opened or closed them. I pulled my backpack into my lap and pulled out my oversized book. The pages ruffled as I turned them.

"Can't you read that later?" my dad asked. "It's not often I get time to drive you to school. I've got a doctor's appointment this morning, so I'm going in late."

"Why are you going to the doctor?" I asked, and stuffed the book back in my bag.

"Well, when you get to be my age, things stop running

so well and you have to get checked up to make sure nothing goes wrong."

"You and mom aren't that old, though," I said, and he laughed. "What could go wrong?"

"Nothing you need to worry about, kid. You're still young."

"Yeah, too young. I'm not even a teenager yet. I can't wait until I'm an adult," I said, and he asked me why. "Well, because then I won't have to deal with all the annoying kids at school, I'll have lots of money, and I'll be able to do whatever I want, whenever I want."

"You think so?" my dad said. "Well, you'll get all the things you want, Stephen, I'm sure. Just take it slow. You're only in seventh grade. Enjoy this time. It's the best time of your life."

"More like the absolute worse time in my life. The other kids are idiots. The day I finish school is the last day any of those jerks will see me again."

"Well, people outgrow stuff. I just worry about you, kid, that's all. I know the kids in school give you a hard time for... well, for the way you are, and the thing is those kids are going to turn into the adults of this town one day, so try to get along with them."

"For what? I'm not staying here," I said. "There's no way I'm staying in this town. My brain needs room to breathe, and it can't do that in this place."

My dad laughed again. We were almost at school. "Well, I just wanted to talk to you about your mom. Has she seemed a little down lately?"

I shrugged. "Down? If anything, that woman is too happy."

"I don't know," he said. "This morning she just seemed distant. Like she was stuck inside of her own head. It's probably nothing, though," he decided.

"Well, maybe you need to step your game up," I said, and thought of all the heroes in my books. They usually did daring things to impress girls. "Do something bold, like take her out on a really nice date. She'd love that. You guys are always doing stuff with me and Warren."

"A nice dinner, huh? She might like that. When we were in school I used to bring her blue sunflowers from the shop downtown. I bet she'd like that too; might get her all nostalgic."

I didn't know what he meant, and I didn't think I was supposed to. But he was smiling, so I stayed quiet and let him think his happy thoughts about days past. The bulbous truck pulled up to the entrance of the middle school.

"Have a great day, and don't let other people's opinions get you down. Those kids wouldn't know genius if it smacked them."

"Thanks, Dad, and thanks for the ride. What time will you be home?"

"Not until late, need to make up for the lost time today, but tell your mom to keep a plate warm for me. And tell Warren I said to stop messing around. Another bad grade and he won't see the sun this summer."

I nodded and shut the door. My dad drove slower than an old lady who was losing her eyesight, so I was surprised I wasn't late. The school was still in its early morning buzz. Car doors opened and shut. Brakes of school buses squealed to a halt. Kids chatted in the courtyard as I limped into the building.

Kids flooded the narrow halls. I saw Trish and Liza waiting by my locker, and I swam toward them—21 steps. There wouldn't be enough time to catch up with them. They could both talk for days without me saying a single word, and I wanted to be early to first period English so I could finish up those last few math problems.

They were already debating something. "What do you think, Stephen?" Liza asked me, and I stared blankly at them.

"Do bullfrogs mate during spring or summer?" Trish asked.

"Spring," I said, and slammed my locker shut. "What's it matter?" They both shrugged. I started to walk away, and they followed me, huddling close to one another.

"We're still on for movies tonight?" Liza asked. "My mom says we can't have it at my house, because she's got another date, which totally sucks because I have dance practice this evening and no one to drive me home."

"I'll ask my mom if she can pick you up, and then she can drive us to Stephen's," Trish said without bothering to ask if it was okay if we had it at my house. She liked being the boss, and I really didn't mind it. Liza and I had a hard time making decisions.

The morning passed before I knew it, and it was already lunch time. Liza, Trish, and I sat out by the bleachers near the courtyard. There were only a few weeks left in the school year, and I couldn't wait for summer. Swimming, fishing, and grilling out by the lake—this was going to be the best summer yet. I needed more books, though, and I had no money to buy them. Warren and I didn't get an allowance, just a few dollars here and there. My mom thought we didn't need money until we started high school. I'd have to cut grass this summer if I didn't want to keep re-reading the same torn-up paperbacks.

Liza and Trish giggled as they aimed grapes at each other's mouths. We were sitting in the grass, and it was still wet from the morning dew. I was done eating, and stretched out on the wet ground with a book in hand. The sun hid behind clouds as the sky rolled by. Warren and Sam the Man sat at the top of the bleachers staring down at us. They munched away on sandwiches and shouted obscene jokes to other kids for their own entertainment. Warren finished his sandwich and hopped down to join us.

"What are you reading?" he asked and sat down. He stared at the massive book in my hand and reached for it. "Can I see it?" I folded down a corner on the page I wanted to return to, and handed him the book. "How do you read this stuff? It's so long."

"It's what I like," I said. "You like hockey. I like science."

"Yeah," he breathed. "I just wish I could read half as much as you do. If I could, maybe I wouldn't be doing so badly in school."

"You're doing fine," I told him. "If you need help, you can always ask me. I did all the same stuff you're doing last year. And it goes both ways. Don't you think I wish I was as good at sports as you are?"

"You don't care about sports," he muttered. "I mean, maybe if your leg wasn't all messed up, you could play too."

"There's nothing wrong with my leg," I said.

"I'm not saying there is. I'm just saying... "

"Well don't say anything." I stood up. "I don't want to hear it," I snapped, and walked away from him. Warren didn't get it, and that pissed me off. He shouldn't have *brought up my limp like that; there wasn't a thing I could do about it, and he knew that.*

*School was over, and Trish sat with me on the steps near the gym. Liza had caught a ride with some girl in her dance class, but Trish's mom would still need to pick her up afterward. We were both waiting on our moms. My mom was running late. She usually got caught up at the grocery store on Thursdays for some reason. It was muggy outside, but not too hot. We were comfortable, and we sat there and talked about everything that didn't matter. Trish gossiped about eighth grade drama—who was dating whom. She loved that stuff, but I couldn't care. She was wearing a dark blue sweater with a big, white cat embroidered on it and a jean skirt. There were big braids in her hair with bobbles tied to the ends.*

*Trish swayed her head back and forth as she got deeper and deeper into her story. Her eyes blazed with excitement over the usual middle school drama. "And then he just left her crying by her locker. Can you believe it? Who dumps somebody in a text message?" She shook her head. "She'll have forgotten all about it, though, once high school starts, I'm sure. No one takes crushes in middle school seriously, right?" she asked.*

*A car horn honked. I saw my mom's burgundy sedan parked near the side of the school. I looked toward it, and she waved at me without smiling.*

*"That's my mom," I stated the obvious. "I'll see you tonight."*

*"How was school?" my mom asked as I climbed in her car. She was wearing her yellow apron from the grocery store, her name tag pinned to it.*

*"Boring," I groaned. She still wasn't smiling, and I won-*

dered if she even heard my reply. "How was work?" I asked. My mom didn't turn to look at me. She stared at the window, and I noticed her shoulders heaving. "Are you alright?" I had no clue what I would do if she said she wasn't, and it was clear that she wasn't. She turned toward me slowly. Her eyes were filled with anguish, tears brimming in the corners. She buried her face in her hands as her body shook with sadness. I sat there in shock. I'd never seen her cry over something that wasn't sappy, and I didn't know what to do. I stayed quiet and placed my hand on her shoulder.

"Mom?" I breathed on a whisper. I was afraid to break the silence.

She finally noticed I was there. "I'm sorry, Stephen." Her voice was cold and robotic. "You shouldn't have had to see that. I'm fine, I really am. Just work stress."

How stressful could being a cashier at a grocery store be? I thought about what my dad had said that morning, and decided he must have been right. She probably felt unappreciated. My dad was nice, but he wasn't the romantic type. The nicest gift he'd ever bought my mom was the Dirt Devil stored in our hall closet.

"Dad loves you," I said. "He loves you, Mom. He's just not that great at showing it."

I thought if I said that it might make her feel better, but it didn't. I could tell she didn't want me to see her so sad, but she cried all the way home. And I felt completely useless.

# CHAPTER 17

# SECRETS REVEALED

THE DREAM FELT more than real, and my mind clung to every memory of my former life. My mom's ringtone was going off in my head. It was some 80s pop song by Cyndi Lauper, and I only remembered the name because of her crazy orange hair and the fact that it was on the soundtrack to the Warner Brother's film *The Goonies*. I thought I was dreaming for sure. But the ringing wouldn't stop. I opened my eyes and took in the clearing, but I could still hear the tune. I glanced over at Trish and Liza, and they weren't moving. They stood away from me, staring down at Trish's dingy jean knapsack.

"It's really ringing," Liza said. "He's calling her. What do we do?"

I jumped up. "Don't answer it, Trish!" I screamed as she moved toward the cell phone. We were all standing around it like it was a bomb. "Please," I begged her. "Just let it go to voicemail, and we'll listen to it, okay?" Trish backed away from her bag as soon as it stopped ringing. We all took in one another's intense facial expressions. They weren't unique. It was obvious we all wanted to grab the phone and listen to the message from my dad.

"Do you want to listen to it first, Stephen?" Liza asked, sounding a lot younger. Her voice was childlike, innocent, and questioning. I didn't respond, but I walked to the phone and picked it up. I hit the voicemail button and listened. Trish and Liza stared at me as if I were listening to all the secrets of adulthood. It felt like time stopped when I recognized my dad's voice. Weeks had passed since I'd last heard it, and it sounded just the same—raspy and unsure. A question hid within each word. He was sobbing, crying, and I hung up the phone.

"What did he say?" Trish asked, and I didn't reply. "Are you going to let us listen to it?" She reached for the phone.

"No." I pulled back from her. "It's too personal. I don't think... I just need a second."

They waited, but they wouldn't tear their eyes away from me. I had to catch my breath.

They grew impatient. "Can you at least tell us what you're thinking?" Trish said.

"He knew," I said. "He knew all this time. She wasn't confessing anything in that letter that he didn't already know. He followed her out one night, and knew that she was being unfaithful. He never said anything, because she got sick. Even when she wrote the letter, he still worried that if he told her what he really thought, it might kill her."

"He loved her so much," Liza said, and she started to cry.

"What else did he say?" Trish asked.

"The last part... it didn't make sense, he was crying so hard. He said he understood why she did it, and that he wanted to forgive her, but he didn't know how. He wants to kill my uncle. There was all this talk about suffering and stolen childhoods. And then he said something about the journal she kept when they were younger."

"Well, he should kill your uncle," Trish said, shocking Liza and me. Any talk of violence made her cringe. "I know you think it's this big secret, but we all know your uncle gets drunk and hits you. He's scum—a complete waste of space."

"Why didn't either of you say anything if you already knew?"

"You didn't want us to know," Liza said. "You've been so secretive lately, and whenever anyone tries to ask you about anything, you shut down."

That was all I knew how to do. I didn't know how to talk about my feelings, and I didn't want there to be any more reasons to pity me.

"What do you want to do now, Stephen?" Trish asked. I wasn't sure what to do. My head was spinning. I couldn't take any more revelations. "I'm sorry we failed. I thought we could change you back. I really thought if we stayed here until dark something would happen. I didn't think we'd still be this far off from a solution."

"Last night, when you guys fell asleep, I saw my mom again. I saw her reflection in the water, and at first she was laughing. It was like nothing had changed, but I couldn't hold back all the resentment I was feeling. I wanted to, but couldn't. And then she started crying, or at least that was what it looked like. It was hard to tell in the dark." They stared at me, and I tried to think back. "And then she mouthed the word 'home.'"

"That's insane. Does that mean we need to go back to your house?" Liza asked. "I mean if we were going to listen to a dead person, that is."

"No, I don't think it means that at all. I think it means we need to go back to her home, the home where she and my uncle grew up. We need to go to Grand Rapids and visit my grandmother."

The only bus that went all the way out to Grand Rapids was about five miles away from Lake Odessa. We would have to walk the long way. The state of Michigan wasn't known for its means of public transportation. We packed up all of our belongings and left the clearing. I left my bike there, hating that I couldn't bring it with me. It might draw too much attention on the bus ride there, and we didn't know how widespread the search for the crazy kid was.

Grandma Rose was the oldest person I knew. The skin on her face looked like sandpaper, and her eyes had a milky white film over them. I never could tell when she was talking to me, and she always mixed me up with Warren. When my mom was alive, we visited Grandma Rose all the time. The house had always smelled like rotting flesh, and hopelessness had a bad habit of lingering in the cracks of the floorboards. It was sad visiting my mom's mom. And it wasn't just sad for me, but it was sad for my mom too. I could tell she didn't like going back there, but she always did, no matter how cross my grandma was toward her.

Grandma Rose was always nice and polite to me and Warren, but my dad told me she wasn't always like that. She had a bad memory and had never been "all there," according to him. I didn't know if that was true, but I knew that house had made my mom sad, and so I thought that maybe if I went there I'd be able to find out why my mom had hated herself. I wanted to place the change she'd experienced, and see if I could prevent it from happening to me. The hate might have started when she cheated, but my instincts were screaming that wasn't it. It could have been my grandma's bad attitude toward her. My grandma needed help, and so within the last year she'd gotten a live-in nurse for herself.

My mom had come from money, not much, but some. Grandma Rose used to be this beautiful lady all the men in town went crazy over. They bought her gifts and gave her money, and she got too used to all the attention. She married for money, and my grandpa died before I ever got to meet him. I'd seen pictures of him, though, and he always looked too old, as if he were holding on to his last dying breath. But I'd been told my grandma was mean to my mom and my uncle when they were growing up, and not just mean, but neglectful too. I knew what that felt like now because I had to put up with my uncle. He didn't possess the power to not put me down. Every time the opportunity presented itself, he took it. He hated me for some reason, and I wasn't sure I wanted to know why.

Neither Trish nor Liza questioned my desire to go there. It felt damning, almost like I was constantly looking for new ways to reopen my wounds. This random act might be just another way to hurt myself. They might have thought that, but they didn't say it. And for that, I was grateful.

We walked the five miles in silence, not knowing what to say to one another. Our emotions turned with each step. I didn't know how much longer I could keep what I was thinking from Trish. I wanted her to know, but I didn't want her to decide to desert me in my time of need. I didn't really believe she would do that. But I knew she wasn't going to like what I was going to say. There was a chance what I wanted to tell her might separate us forever.

The bus was packed with bodies when we got on. There was one empty seat up front, and the only other one was against the back of the bus. I let Trish and Liza take the seat up front, and I took the one in the back. I slid in next to a man wearing hiking boots and a beanie on his head. He had a gray beard and a head of white hair. He smiled at me as I sat down, but I didn't smile back. My brain moved too slowly to even consider what I should do in return.

Trish glanced back at me from the front row. I caught her looking, but she didn't turn away. There wasn't any way to get away from Trish. We lived too close to one another, and I would never stop having to see her in school. The feeling of hurt that returned whenever she looked at me wouldn't fade easily. The sting of rejection burned my throat, and she hadn't considered how it would make me feel. I knew she cared about me. But I couldn't take this, being in her presence and pretending. This was insanity, and it would have to stop.

We reached the closest stop to Grandma Rose's home and got off the bus. Trish and Liza stood there waiting for me to get off. I walked off from them, and Trish grabbed my arm.

"You can stop being mad at me now," she said, and I was silent. "Please?"

"It doesn't work like that, Trish. I won't always be here to do everything you say."

"Of course you will," she said. "They're not going to take you to jail, Stephen, if that's what you're worrying about. Look, I know you're scared, and I know you're pissed at me for texting your dad. But you'll thank me for it later."

"Yeah, I'll thank you when I'm visiting my dad in a mental hospital. Maybe I'll get lucky and they'll lock us up in the same one."

"Don't be ridiculous!" Trish shouted. "They don't let children and adults attend the same mental institutions."

"Let's just keep walking. My tongue's too tired to keep talking, and my grandma's house is this way," I told her, ignoring her words. The familiar streets brought an aching to my chest. These were the streets Warren and I had tossed a football on last Thanksgiving. Grandma Rose hadn't cooked for us, but had it catered instead. My mom had brought her famous pumpkin cheesecake and salted malt chocolate muffins. Antique houses filled the road, but the best thing about that street was the streetlamps. They looked like they'd come from London or Paris.

Mirabelle, my grandma's nurse, answered the door when we knocked. I thought she might be shocked to see me standing there, but she looked bored as she ushered the three of us in from the cold. Sorrow gripped me by the throat as I stepped into the formal living room. It was clad in elegant white furniture with white damask patterns. The living room looked like a white canvas, cold and unfeeling like an expensive museum. This was what I hated about coming here. Everything was white and fragile; it wasn't a place for children.

We sat on the pristine white couch while Mirabelle went to collect Grandma Rose. She couldn't walk, so the nurse pushed her into the living room in a wheelchair. Her sickness had grown more severe since my mom had died. Mirabelle put the wheelchair next to the fireplace. Grandma Rose hunched over in her seat without saying a word.

"Who's there?" she asked. The film on her eyes was even thicker now. I knew she couldn't see me, even though I sat only a few feet away from the fireplace.

"It's Stephen," I said, getting up from the couch so she could get a better look at the shape of my face, "your oldest grandson."

"Darling," she crooned. "Can you get me some coffee and biscuits? I'm very hungry and tired and would really like some coffee and biscuits. Won't you please fetch them for me, dear?" She always wanted someone to do something for her. I looked toward Mirabelle. She nodded and made her way to the kitchen for the requested coffee and biscuits. "Where's my pretty Daisy?" she asked. I didn't respond. "Where's your mom?" she asked again. Her memory was getting worse, too, and I was not going to remind her that my mom had died over a month ago.

"She's at work," I lied. "They're doing a toy drive at

the church. She asked me to come out here to get some of her old dolls. We don't want to bother you."

"Who's we? Where's Daisy?" she said again.

"Me and my friends," I said and motioned toward Trish and Liza. They were trying their best to not look directly at anything. "Daisy's at work, remember?" She didn't say anything. "Can we get the dolls for the toy drive?"

"Yes, child," she snapped in her fragile voice. "Go get your mom's dolls. Don't know why she thinks they're hers. I bought her those damn dolls," she said. "You know where her room is. I'm going to take a nap, so you keep quiet," she muttered, and called to Mirabelle to take her to her bedroom.

"Your grandma is super strange," Liza said. "I almost feel bad for your uncle."

"Yeah, well don't."

The door to my uncle's childhood bedroom had always stayed locked, but my mom's was wide open. The room was all done up in lace and antique-looking floral patterns. It was still white, just like the rest of the house. The room looked like it hadn't changed much, besides my grandma storing more junk in it. There were several packing boxes in the corner by the bed, and my grandma's old clothes and fancy winter coats filled the closet. I pulled down a box from the top shelf that was filled with my mom's old glass dolls.

"You're really taking those?" Liza asked.

I nodded. "Might as well. They'll just end up in some donation box. I think they belong in our house anyway. My mom loved these ugly things." I held one in my hand

and stared at the creepy glass eyes. Liza helped me move the box and sort through a few of the dolls that had seen better days.

"Can I keep one?" she asked. "I've never seen a glass doll before."

"Sure, why not," I said. We both stopped moving when we noticed Trish wasn't standing near the closet with us. We looked around the room for her and saw her crouched between my mom's nightstand and her four-poster bed. I stared down at her hands, and she held a worn plastic book with a big plastic heart for a lock. It was my mom's diary, and whatever Trish had read was making her cry. I knew I needed to ask her why she was crying, but somewhere in the pit of my stomach, I already knew the reason.

# THE MONSTER

I GRABBED MY MOM'S diary out of Trish's hands and sat down on the bed to read it. Every inch of my mind screamed out in warning. I touched the vein on my temple as it pulsed and throbbed. My mind was on overload. "Don't!" Trish screamed. "Please don't read it. Your mom wouldn't want anyone to read this, ever. We need to burn it."

There was no turning back now since we'd come all this way. I ignored Trish and opened the small book to the space where she'd been reading. The entry was dated September 15, 1985. My brain calculated backward, and I deducted that my mom had been twelve years old when she wrote this, and my uncle would have been sixteen at the time.

\*

*There's a monster that lives in my home. His shadow lurks at my bedroom door. He seeks me out when the sun*

*goes down, always knowing where to find me. He hides
in dark corners, under rocks and beyond bends, staying
hidden. The monster waits until we're all alone. Then he
frightens me with his slithering snake voice and his scaly
white hands. He pins me down. He won't let me fight.*

*The monster haunts my every move. I cannot escape no
matter how hard I try. He follows me home from school
and out to the grocery store. Wherever I look the monster
is there. He hides behind bushes and watches me get
on the bus to school. When I try to fight, he smacks me,
punches me, leaving marks on my face and arms.*

*When I wake, he sits at our kitchen table eating
breakfast, staring at me. He watches my body, but not my
face. I feel his eyes on me as they burn away my insides.
He touches me at night, in the dark as I lay in my bed. I
lock the door, but it doesn't keep him out. Nothing does.*

*The monster hates me. He wants me to die. He comes
out from the shadows and smirks like a baby. His hairy,
sweaty monster hand covers my mouth so no one hears
me scream. He buries himself inside me, leaving blood on
my bed sheets.*

*My mom—she doesn't believe me. She says the monster
isn't real. He's just a bad dream that I can't escape. But
he is real, and he won't stop hurting me. The monster's
bigger and stronger than me. He laughs when I fight and
smiles when I cry.*

*The monster torments me when I stay home sick from
school. He hides until my mom's gone, and binds me,*

*tortures me. I scream and cry, beg and plead, but the monster doesn't care. He only wants more. Nothing is ever enough. He won't ever stop.*

*I hide from the monster that sleeps down the hall, but he always finds me. He stumbles in late at night when my momma's sleeping, tripping on his over-sized monster feet. I hear him as he walks toward my bedroom and his hand reaches for the door. I want to disappear so the monster can't find me here.*

*I can't save myself. The monster says he can't stop hurting me. He tells me it's my fault that he exists. He says I made him this way. The monster hates me, but no more than I hate myself. There's no one who can save me from my monster. My feet won't outrun him. The monster will stay with me for the rest of my life.*

\*

The childhood version of my mom hadn't written any other similar entries in the plastic journal. I flipped through the pages looking for something more, anything else that could tell me why she had written this. But everything else in the pink diary was about school and friends, lunch dates and violin lessons. The life the rest of the journal painted didn't match that last entry. I wondered if my mom wrote this so my grandma could find it and maybe then she would believe the monster had been real. I knew what all of it meant, but I was afraid to put the pieces together, afraid of what had been done to my mom and to know who the monster was. No one should have a childhood like that, but it had been my mom's reality—living with a monster. Living with my uncle, I knew what it was like, but he hadn't hurt me the way he had hurt my mom. He'd beaten me, tortured me, and kicked me when I was down, but that paled in comparison to what my mom had experienced growing up.

I had always known there was something wrong with my uncle—he was violent, vengeful, and just plain stupid. Hurting other people brought him pleasure, and I couldn't understand how someone ended up like that. Or how he functioned without feeling any guilt or sadness over my mom's death. I had searched his eyes, a time or two, looking for a sense of remorse, but found nothing. It was he who had been the most unaffected by her death, and now I could see why. My mom died with his secret. She had been the weight he carried, and now she was gone. He hated me because he hated her. But he had been the one to destroy her life and his own.

My chest burned, like flames melting away the rims of my ribcage. The heat wouldn't stop. I felt it rise to my throat, and I knew I needed to get out of this house. This bed, this was the bed where my uncle had raped my mom when she was only twelve years old. The act, that kind of hate, was something I didn't want to ever understand, but I wanted my uncle to suffer for killing my mom in such a slow and tortuous way. He did that to her. He hurt her and stole her chance at happiness to prove he was powerful.

"Stephen," Trish called, dragging out my name with caution. She stared down at the diary as it shook in my hands. "Are you going to say anything?" she asked me, and I couldn't reply. My voice was lost. It hid within the walls of this detrimental home. I wanted to watch it burn to the ground, along with my grandma. She hadn't protected my mom, and all my mom had ever cared about was being good enough for her.

The room started to spin as I thought about Warren being alone with my uncle. I pictured my mom sleeping in this bed, crying, waiting for him to come in and hurt her while my grandma slept across the hall. How could she not have known? As I sat on the bed, I stared out the one window that faced the street. This was where she had grown up. This was where my uncle had tortured her again, and again. She must have forgiven him at some point, thought him a changed man and let him into our house. And Dad knew—he had known all along that my uncle had raped my mom when she was little, yet he still hadn't tried to save me and Warren from him. No one had been there to protect my mom just as there had been no one to protect me.

The diary burned my fingers and caught fire in my hands. It shot out from my grip and through the window, smashing it. The sound of glass breaking echoed throughout the silent home. I got up from the bed and took in every detail of that bedroom. My chest heaved as the room started to quake. The books on the floating shelves quivered, and the glass dolls fell to the floor, shattering.

"Stop it, Stephen," Liza said. "You're making the house shake. You're going to wake up your grandma."

But I couldn't stop. There was no way to control the hurt I felt. My mom's pain burned inside me. She was dead now, and she'd never had any redemption. She deserved it, and I would be the one to get it for her.

Trish tried to stop me when the lamp smashed into

a bedroom wall. She reached for me, but it didn't matter. My mind couldn't be stopped. Every object in the room broke against a surface, and I was the one causing it. The room had to be destroyed. The house had to be destroyed. I could hear my grandma shouting to Mirabelle. She screamed about an earthquake and begged Mirabelle to save Kasey and Daisy. I ran out of my mom's old bedroom and down the hall to where the monster had once lived.

I kicked the door down. I didn't look over my shoulder for Trish or Liza. Mirabelle stood in the hall watching my destruction. I don't know what I expected to find in my uncle's room—an awful cave or an actual goblin costume that he used to frighten my mom? There was nothing there but a teenager's room. It could have just as easily belonged to me or Warren. Posters of 80s rock bands dressed as scantily clad women coated the walls. A record player and piles of old comic books sat under the window next to the bedside table. I searched for something that would give away the fact that he was a child rapist, but there was nothing, so I destroyed the room just like my mom's.

Cracks ran down the walls as the home's structure weakened. I shouted to Mirabelle to get my grandma out of the house. I focused my thoughts on the old stove in the kitchen. My emotions fueled the heat, causing the gas line to break. Trish and Liza ran out the front door at my urging. I helped Mirabelle carry my decaying grandma into the yard, and we watched as the house burned down to the ground.

Sirens wailed down the streets once the firemen and cops began to arrive on the scene. They came with hoses of water, but the fire wouldn't stop. I wouldn't let it. The house burned as I controlled the fire, and Trish, Liza, and I used the chaos to mask our departure.

We walked as far off from the house as we could. Trish and Liza wouldn't speak to me; they only whispered to one another. They were worried, frightened about what I'd just done. But now was not the time for fear. I knew what needed to happen. I listened as Trish recounted for Liza what she had read in my mom's diary. It was even harder to hear the second time, so I tried to block it out. Liza didn't ask for any elaborations, and I was glad about it. I couldn't take any more, and I needed to get home.

"Can we stop for a minute?" Liza asked. "Where are we going?"

I hadn't been paying attention to the path we followed. All that mattered was that I kept walking. I had to get to him. He was going to admit to what he'd done. The words in that diary were floating in and out of my brain. I couldn't stop re-reading it, growing more and more frustrated with each thought. There was a sharp aching in my sternum, and I stopped in my tracks. I gripped my chest and watched as Trish's mouth flew open in shock. I sat down on the edge of the street, trying to catch my breath. My whole body shook, and I couldn't stop the sounds that were coming out of my mouth.

"Calm down. Please, calm down, Stephen, or you're going to have a heart attack," Trish said. "Everything's going to be fine. I promise it will be. Just calm down. I need you," she said. And I was able to slow my beating heart. I sucked in air and waited before moving again. "How do you feel?" she asked me.

"Like I could spit fire," I said to her, and she laughed.

"You might just be able to," Liza said without humor. "That was the craziest, scariest thing I've ever seen in my life. And you did it, Stephen. You caused all of that." Liza whistled.

"I don't want to be like this anymore," I told them. "We have to find out how to change me back, or I'm going to explode."

"We will," Trish said. "We're going to figure this out, and nothing like that is ever going to happen again. This has to stop."

"No," I said. My abilities made me feel strong; I would need them intact when I saw him. He wasn't going to hurt me again. He wouldn't ever hurt anyone again, and I had to make that true. I had to. "We can't stop it now. I have to go home first. We need to save Warren from my uncle. He has to admit what he did to my mom. I'm taking my house back."

They stared at me in silence. Trish moved to sit down next to me on the street curb. Her words were so careful, it almost made me lose my mind.

"Do you really want to see him again, now that we know what happened?"

"You read what he did, Trish. He should be in jail. Something has to be done about this. We can't just let him off the hook. It's the most horrific thing I've ever heard. She couldn't escape him. He lived in her house, and he raped her whenever the hell he felt like it. It's worse than being his punching bag. It's the worst thing I could ever imagine." My chest was starting to get warm again as I imagined my twelve-year-old mom cowering in fear from a dark and shapeless figure.

"I hate him too," she said. "Not as much as you do, but I hate him for what he did to her. I just don't know if we were meant to find out this way. I don't know if there's anything we can do now that she's dead and you destroyed the diary."

"There has to be something," I cried. "Please, Trish, tell me there's something we can do so he goes to jail."

"Well, from what I've read, people like your uncle don't usually go to jail for stuff like this. We need witnesses, and your mom never told anyone."

I thought for a moment. "That's not true. She told my dad. My dad knew."

"But what did he know?" she asked. "We don't know how deep this goes."

"My grandma, she knew. She had to!" I screamed then paused as I tried to control myself. My heart fluttered, causing an ache in my left shoulder. I rubbed the space, but it wouldn't stop the pain. "She knew, Trish. She knew all this time, and she never did anything, because she wanted to protect Kasey. That's all she ever cared about. She never cared about my mom." I wanted to cry. I knew what that felt like. My mom and I didn't have much in common, but we shared that pain, the pain of feeling like you could die and the world might not notice your passing.

"What are the chances of her telling the truth about it now?" Trish asked. "She's not a viable witness. She's lost her memory, and she's losing her mind. They aren't going to listen to her, and as for your dad—all he can do is repeat what your mom told him."

"I can't let this go, you guys. I can't. I have to stand up to him. He needs to suffer for what he did. He deserves to know what it feels like to hurt. I have to go home and face him. Take my house back. I'd rather go into foster care than to have to live with him again."

"We'll go with you," Trish said. "We'll help you stand up to him. Your mom would have wanted us to do that."

## CHAPTER 19

# COMING HOME

T HE STREETS WE crossed blurred in my vision. Words, sights, and sounds all blended into the background of my mind. We said nothing to each other as we dredged along to the nearest bus stop. There weren't words to describe the pain; I felt like I could hear my mom calling me home from our front door as I played on the streets. I could see the street lights in my mind, the familiar rows of house, our cracked driveway, and my mom's dark brown hair framed in the doorway. The light shined behind her. She was calling me, calling me home.

Everything fell into place—the way she raised me, the way my uncle watched her with fear and resentment in his eyes, the tone of his voice whenever he mentioned her, and the fact that he never would say her name. My father never got too close to my uncle. He always kept his distance. And while all of these things ran through my mind, I still managed to catch Trish staring at me. We still needed to talk, but I couldn't focus on something so small.

My memory of that day at the fair was tiny as it stood in a corner of my clouded mind. But even though I couldn't admit much to myself, I knew I was going through with confronting my uncle.

We got on the bus, and Liza sat down in the first row of seats, leaving me and Trish to sit together in the open seat behind her. I didn't know if I should try to talk to her, and I imagined she was thinking the same thing. She wanted to say something, I could tell, but she was struggling within herself, not wanting to trivialize everything else. I turned to her, opening my mouth to speak, then shut it, thinking better of it.

She caught me. "Do you want to say something to me?" she asked. I shook my head. "Look, I know this is all happening at a rapid pace, and we haven't talked about anything, the night at the fair or anything, and I just wanted to say that it was the best night of my life." She paused and stared out the window of the bus. I wanted her to look at me. I wanted to see her face, but I didn't ask her to turn toward me. "I can't even tell you how long I'd been hoping you would notice me, Stephen—since we were little, I guess. I've always seen you as this over-the-top smart and super sweet guy. There's no one else at school who cares so little about the perceptions of others. It's just strange to me, and that's always what pulled me to you. There are a lot of people out there who would have used the limp as an excuse, but you used it as fuel to be different, to be better, and I just… I don't know. It's a mystery to me, and so when we kissed, it was something I wanted, but it also confused the hell out of me."

Finally, she looked at me as her words thickened the

atmosphere between us. The words were hanging there, waiting for her to continue, but she didn't. "What is it, Trish?" I said.

"I'm just scared," she muttered. "I don't want to lose you. You're my best friend, and I don't want a crush ruining that. I don't want anything to change."

"It doesn't have to," I said.

"Oh, but it does. We can't hurt Liza." She whispered, but Liza jumped up and faced us.

"What would hurt me?" Liza asked. We stared at her with guilt-stricken eyes.

I wanted to be bold. "Do you have a crush on me, Liza?"

She shot a glare at Trish and then burst into laughter. "Are you kidding me, Patricia Adams? I cannot believe you." Liza punched Trish in the shoulder. "You are so obsessed with Stephen, it's beyond me." She shook her head in disbelief. "I was only joking when I said that. You've had a crush on him forever, and I just wanted to mess with you. You know, keep you on your toes and all that." She laughed, and I thought Trish was going to strangle her.

"I hate you, Elizabeth Thomas! I hate you more than anything! How could you embarrass me like that? Do you know I've been stirring over betraying you this entire time?"

"Oh, I love you too. It was just a joke; calm down," Liza said. "I really do love you, Trish. I'm sorry. I thought you knew I was joking when I said it."

Trish muttered something under her breath and pushed her back further into her seat.

"Trish? Trish? My love?" Liza said, trying to meet Trish's eyes. "You'll thank me later." She smiled and turned around in her seat.

I moved closer to Trish and wrapped my arms around her waist, pulling her toward me. At first, she resisted, but eventually she melted into me.

"We don't have to make this anything if you don't want to," I said. "We're still in middle school, and I just feel like we have all the time in the world to argue over what should happen between us. I just want you around, Trish. That really is enough for me. Things can stay the same, and I'll keep my feelings to myself, but they are there. I want you to know I really care about you—I mean like a lot. I won't go into detail, because I don't want to weird you out." She smiled as I kept talking. "But that night at the fair was the best night of my life too. I do think it will be hard to go back to just being friends, but if that's what you want, then who am I to push you away? I just want you to be considerate of me. It's going to hurt, watching guys line up to date you while I've been relegated to the friend zone."

"That won't happen, Stephen. I wouldn't hurt you, and I don't know if I'd be able to date anyone like that. I'm just not interested. I like you, but this just happened. There are so many things I want in this life other than a boyfriend. Boyfriends are my least concern. But you, you'll always be there. And I'll always be here for you too."

I nodded, and she rested her head on my shoulder. It felt perfect, and it didn't matter what the future brought. Trish knew how I felt, and I knew how she felt, and that was enough. She was my best friend, and that wouldn't ever change. She was my future—even though I didn't know what my future would be, I knew she'd be in it. Liza would be there too. I needed my best friends. And even though things were completely screwed up, in that instant, everything felt like a storm reaching its calm. This was my happiness. Knowing that the three of us would never part was all I needed to find my strength.

The bus dropped us off on the outskirts of Lake Odessa, near the freeway. Trish announced that she forgave Liza, but made her promise to not play jokes like that again. Liza said she wouldn't, but we all knew that was a lie. I stared down at my scuffed and torn red Converses. It seemed they had a mind of their own as we walked toward my familiar street. There were only a few streets in our small town, and it was miraculous that we had all ended up living so close together. It was meant to be. I'd felt so betrayed by my mom's loss, but it was meant to happen. I thought about how selfish I'd been, but I didn't regret it. I couldn't think of any way to not be selfish when something like this happened. My thoughts turned to my dad.

My dad loved me. He loved Warren. But more than anything else, he loved my mom. She had held his world in her tiny palm, and now she was gone. I started to think about how that might feel, and what Trish had said about him not wanting to go back to that house—it made sense. But now there was nothing I wanted more than to come home. It wasn't fair that cancer had stolen my mom. It wasn't fair that she'd been born into a family with a rapist for a brother. It wasn't fair that I had been born with a limp, but life's not fair. You get what you get in this world.

You make the most of it and try to find those few good things that somehow overshadow the bad.

There were two cop cars parked on either side of our street as we approached my house. I felt cold, and my instinct was to numb myself to what I was about to do, but I didn't. I needed to be present. I needed to make sure my uncle understood the seriousness of what he'd done and that I wasn't going to let him hurt anyone ever again.

It was close to nightfall. We hid near the bushes outside of Liza's house, and I saw my uncle's car parked in our driveway. We ducked behind fences and cars, trying to stay hidden, but as we neared my driveway we saw that both of the police cars were empty. We didn't get too close, but we could see that no one sat inside either one.

"They must have parked them here to keep you from coming home," Trish guessed. That didn't make much sense, but it had worked in our favor. We crept up to my uncle's car and used it to mask our figures.

"Are you just going to walk inside and confront him?" Trish asked, her voice quivering as she tried to mask her nervousness. I didn't know what to do now. I was afraid to go inside that house. The light shined in Warren's bedroom, and every now and then the TV room flashed from the flickering of the television. Dark clouds filled the sky as water droplets clung to our skin and clothes. The rain pattered upon the pavement, and I knew we would need a distraction if we had any chance of getting inside the house without my uncle noticing.

I motioned for Trish and Liza to follow me to the side of the garage. We crouched down on the ground, and I peered around the siding to focus on my uncle's car. All four car windows exploded at the same time. The glass erupted with a bang, and my uncle raced down the front porch and into the driveway. The noise distracted him, just like I wanted. The three of us snuck around to the back porch. The door was locked, and when I reached inside my pocket for the key there was nothing there. Liza stomped her foot in frustration. "Damn it," she whispered. And there was a rap on the glass sliding door.

Warren stood there, staring at us with fear in his eyes. He looked down at the lock on the door and then back up at me.

"Let me in," I told him, but he didn't move. "Warren," I spoke softly, "please let me in the house. I want to come home." We all watched as his right hand lowered and unlocked the door. He pushed back the glass and let us inside.

"What happened to you?" he asked me. "I didn't think you would come back here. You know the cops are looking for you. It was pretty stupid to come home."

"I came home to save you," I said and expected him to laugh at the dramatics in my words. But he didn't. He stood there staring at me. Then he moved in close and wrapped his arms around me, embracing me for the first time in months. He started to cry, and I let him. We all stood there between the kitchen and the TV room listening as my brother sobbed for what felt like days. He had changed in the two short days since my clumsy escape.

"I'm here. I'm not going anywhere," I told him. "I had to go, but I wouldn't leave you here with him. I love you, you little snot."

Warren grumbled something that sounded like "I love

you too." I wasn't sure if that's what he said, but I pretended it was because that was what I wanted to hear. He stepped back from me, and I stayed quiet and still. "I'm sorry I was such an ass," he said. "I just felt like no one understood, and I was so pissed about everything—about the cancer, about Dad leaving. I didn't want to look like a kid, but I didn't know what to say or how to feel. I just... I'm sorry. And you were right: I do miss her. I never stopped missing her."

"Whatever, kid," I said. "You know I'm always going to be here no matter what. You're all the family I have."

"What about Uncle Kasey?" he asked. "Since you left he's been starting fights with me every night. I thought he was going to kill me last night. He wanted me to make dinner, and when I couldn't, he just started throwing shit and screaming at me."

"He's leaving here tonight," I said, reminding myself just how much I'd changed since that night in the clearing. "Lock the front door. That asshole is not coming back in this house. Not without a fight."

Warren locked the front door, and I peered out the window to see my uncle standing in the driveway wearing his work jeans and wife-beater. He looked like an oversized walrus stuffed into a people suit. He teetered back and forth, from one leg to the other, inspecting his car and trying to figure out what had gone wrong. He didn't look toward the front window, and so he didn't notice the extra shadows moving in the light. I used my mind to rock the car from left to right, side to side, back and forth to confuse him further. He kneeled down on the ground, and when the car shook, he jumped up and looked around.

His eyes sought the front window. He saw me standing there, and he clunked his boots up to the front door. Our eyes locked, but I didn't move.

His fists pounded on the front door. The four of us waited. We listened as he tried to kick the door down. The sound of his foot hitting the dense wood made us jump. Every kick made us jump. He shouted my name, threatening to kill me and call the police.

"Open this door, you fucking psycho," he screamed at me. "You little piece of shit. Just wait until I get my hands around your scrawny throat. You are going to die! Do you hear me, gimpy? I'm going to fucking kill you!" His words rang in our ears, but not one sound did we make. I was determined to let him sweat. I wanted him livid when he faced me. "Warren!" my uncle called to my kid brother. "If you don't open this fucking door, I'm going to kill you too! I'll beat your face in until your eyes are so swollen you won't see a damn thing." Warren stayed silent, and my uncle kicked the door again. "I'm going to rip your goddamn arms off!" he shouted in frustration.

There was a slur in his voice. I glanced at the time from the digital readout on the microwave in our kitchen. It was only 6:15 and he had already bathed his liver in alcohol. The pounding against the door stopped. And I listened as the sound of his steel-toe boots made their way to the back of the house. We saw him standing on the back porch, looking in through the door, but we couldn't hear him through the glass. He wore his malicious, child-like grin. His mouth didn't move, but when I looked down, he held a heavy wrench in his hands. He must have grabbed it when he was fooling around with his car. He tossed it up and down and then flung it at the back door, shattering the glass. The sound echoed through the night, and Trish let out a chilling screech.

My heart rate picked up as I watched him getting closer to us. He really wanted to kill me and Warren. It was there on his face, hanging like drool from the corner of his lips. The clunking of those boots was a sound I wouldn't ever forget. It always sent a certain terror through my veins. Fear was starting to set in. My uncle was a big guy; I couldn't do this. He was going to kill me. I stood there watching him walk toward me as every cell in my body was telling me to run, to survive.

"You can do this. Don't forget," Trish whispered. "Don't forget about your mom."

He raced through the back door and lunged at me. I dodged him and used my mind to throw a beer bottle from the end table at his head. My powers moved every object they could grasp, and I sent them flying toward him. He fell to the ground when the bottle struck him, and he reached for my feet, trying to pull me down with him. The length of my legs weighed me down, and I fell. I screamed at Trish and Liza to run as my uncle pummeled my face with his fists. They dashed out the back door, but Warren stayed. I tasted blood, and I could hear someone shouting. I saw Warren jump on my uncle's back, trying to save me.

"Don't, Warren!" I shouted and used my mind to fling my uncle's body off me. He and Warren crashed into the television. I watched as he grabbed Warren in a chokehold. There was something sharp in his hands. The metal glinted in the dark. He held the box cutter we kept on the top of the bookshelf.

"Do any more of that freaky shit, and I will cut his fucking eyes out so you can watch, gimpy." He breathed like a madman, nostrils flaring. I jumped as lightning struck the street outside. Even the cracking thunder couldn't break the tension.

## CHAPTER 20

# THUNDER AND LIGHTNING

THE OBJECTS I'D been controlling fell to the carpeted floor—books, DVDs, bottles, and the television remote. My uncle gripped Warren with one hand and the box cutter with the other. Our staggered breath sounded over the crashing thunder outside the door. Lightning broke through the blackness of the old house. I felt faint from all the mental strain, but I wouldn't let my uncle see me sweat. He wanted me to shake in fear, but I wasn't going to give in to him.

"The cops are on their way to haul you off to the loony bin, you fucking psycho," my uncle said, holding on to Warren.

"Good, let them come," I told him. I knew the cops weren't on their way. He'd had no time to call them. He was stalling, and I was going to let him. The confession I wanted would fall from his lips. I just needed to push him to the top of the steeple, and then he'd tumble over all on his own. "They'll arrest you before they even notice me."

Uncle Kasey scoffed. "You idiot, the whole damn town's been searching for your limping ass. They're going to be thrilled when they catch the town freak!"

"I'm sure they'd rather arrest a child rapist than some telepathic pre-teen," I said through gritted teeth.

His faced turned to hardened stone as he set his jaw. "What the hell are you talking about?" he growled. Warren struggled to get free, and Uncle Kasey flailed his body to keep him still.

I kept my eyes on Warren's as I spoke to my uncle. I wasn't going to let him hurt Warren. "Scared now, huh?" I teased him. "I bet you thought no one would ever find out. I'm sure you really believed that my mom hadn't ever told anyone and that even if she did no one would believe her. Your word over hers, right?"

"Shut the fuck up, you little shit." I could see the hatred seething in his eyes. Even now that she was dead he still despised her. "You don't know what you're talking about. Your mom was a stupid little bitch who got everything she wanted." He spat. "My mom thought she was God's fucking gift." He paused to snarl at me through his rotting teeth. "She was nothing but a slut! She fucked every guy in town."

"I won't shut up, because you did it! Admit it, you asshole. You raped my mom." The words came out flat, leaving an aching in my heart. And I felt the little light jump inside me.

He laughed. "Did that senile old bat tell you that? She's too old to remember anything your mom said. And so what if something did happen when we were kids. Your mom's fucking dead; no one cares what happened now."

"This is her house! This is my home. You need to leave. Just leave us the fuck alone! There's no reason for you to stay here, sleeping in her bed every night when you know what you did. How the hell could you do something like that?" I was crying. Warren was crying. My uncle just kept spitting and shouting, trying to reason with himself.

"What the hell's it matter now? What's done is fucking done! Look, I was a messed up teenager, and I might have did some shit to your mom when I was drunk, but I don't remember it now. And I don't give a shit about it anymore! I'm not leaving. You're fucking stuck with me, gimpy. Now hand me the damn phone. I'm calling the cops so they can take you the fuck away."

I wanted to kill him, but I didn't want Warren to get hurt in the process. "I'm not doing a damn thing for you. You're fucking scum. What kind of worthless piece of shit rapes his kid sister when his mom's sleeping?"

"I never raped anybody. You better shut the fuck up, or I'm going to cut your fucking brother. Is that what you want? You want to watch him suffer?"

"Let him go," I said, trying to hide just how defeated I felt. "He's just a kid."

"So are you, gimpy. You really think you can take me? Not without your freaky shit, you can't. I will kill you," he breathed. "No one would even know."

I watched as the box cutter moved closer to Warren's flesh. My mind was still weak, but I used it to throw the box cutter across the room and away from my uncle. He released Warren and stared at the floating object. Warren ran out the back door, moving through the trees, just as Trish and Liza had done moments before. It was just me and my uncle now, and he really thought it would be easy to kill me. I thought he would grab for Warren, but he didn't. He just stared at me.

"The police know. If you call them, they're just going to take you to jail."

He laughed again. "They don't know shit, you little liar. Your mom never told anyone."

"My dad knows," I said, finding my courage.

"Your dad's the biggest punk I've ever fucking met. Where is he, kid? Is he going to come save you?" Uncle Kasey asked as he moved in on me. He had me trapped in a corner near the front door and the coat closet. His right elbow struck me in the chest, pinning me against the wall. I looked up at him as he stared down at me.

"Just admit it," I said. "Admit what you did."

"I already told you I'm not admitting to shit. Your mom's fucking dead, kid. What does it matter, huh?" He slammed me into the wall. "Tell me what difference it makes." He punched me in the jaw. My head moved with the swift blow. My face burned, but I turned my head back to face him. I was more of a man than he would ever be.

"She forgave you, didn't she?" I asked. "You came into her room and raped her when she was only twelve. She lived in fear because of you!" I spat. "And she still took you in. Why doesn't it matter to you?" I cried. "It made her crazy. She hated herself because of you. She died with your secret, and all you've done in return is move from torturing her in the worst way to beating her sons. I hope you die," I said as the heat burned in my chest. The room swayed, and the house shook from my anger, from my hurt. The ground rumbled as the thunder and lightning darted back and forth in the night sky.

"Stop it," my uncle said, pushing his elbow further into my collar bone. "Stop it right fucking now, or I'm going to strangle you." He reached his hands around my neck, and I kicked him in the shin before he could get a strong grip. He reached for his shin, and I took off for the back door, racing through the small yellow kitchen. I ran as fast as I could, but he flung me against the row of kitchen cabinets. My right knee shattered as I hit the counter. My uncle punched me three times before I hit the floor. My vision blurred, but I could still see Uncle Kasey towering over me.

"Learn to walk, you fucking cripple," he spat. And I stayed quiet, just as I always did. I felt myself falling back through time, back to a time when my mind trembled in panic at the sound of his voice. He kicked me in my gut, waited for me to feel a sense of relief, and then kicked me in the back of my head. I heard him laugh before his foot collided with my face. Warm liquid pooled over my face and down my head. I tried to climb off the floor, but he jumped me and started slamming my head into the linoleum. Each time, my vision grew blurrier. He was going to kill me. I was going to die on the kitchen floor of my own home, and there wasn't anyone to save me.

I felt like I was screaming for help, but my lungs burned. The kitchen lights flickered on and off. It was all too much. I felt my mind disintegrating with each glimmer. The heat took over. My uncle jumped back as if the heat in my chest had burned him. I could hear a thudding sound, a scrambling of boots across the hardwood floors.

My body convulsed as congealed blood crept into the corners of my eyes. And then I could hear my dad. I could hear him shouting. It was just like when I had heard my mom in the clearing, but my dad wasn't dead. His voice ricocheted in my mind. I focused on the sound of him calling my name. He was trying to get to me, but he seemed too far away.

Everything was lost, including my mind. My body stopped flailing, and I was able to open my eyes. I touched my head, and it was still bleeding. The lights had gone out. It was pitch black in the kitchen, and my uncle was gone. My eyes darted around the kitchen, but I couldn't see him. I didn't sense his threatening presence, but when I looked up finally, I saw him.

Not my uncle, but my dad.

My dad was standing there wearing the same clothes he'd had on that day in the hospital. He hadn't shaved in months, and he'd lost at least fifteen pounds. More wrinkles had formed around the corners of his eyes. He looked like he'd been on a crying binge. Staring at him was like looking at a beam of light, a surge of hope, despite his haggard appearance. I felt like I'd aged ten years since I saw him last. I felt like a man now.

"Can you breathe?" my dad asked me. I tried to sit up. "Don't move," he said. "You're bleeding everywhere. What happened to you? I should have called. I should have come back," he scolded himself. "Where the hell is Kasey? He's supposed to be keeping an eye on you, and just look at you. Who did this?"

"Dad, don't," I said. "I'm fine. Everything's fine. I can't believe you came back." I steadied myself to a sitting position and hugged him. He smelled like a stale motel room. Then my fear returned. "Where's Uncle Kasey?"

"I just asked you that, kiddo," he said, still embracing me. I shook him off and looked up at him. "Did someone break in here while he was out at the bar? I told your mom he was going to go back to drinking. I shouldn't have believed him when he said everything was fine here."

"You called?" I asked.

"Of course I called. Your uncle said you and Warren were too pissed to talk to me, so I figured I'd make it up to you two when I got home. You didn't think I would come back?"

"I thought you'd deserted us," I said. "I didn't know you were calling. I didn't think you cared about us anymore."

"You two are all I have left in this world. I was going to come back sooner, but every day I spent away made it harder and harder to come back. I couldn't stand the looks. Being in this house..." A sob broke through his chest. "It doesn't feel like I thought it would. I thought I'd come into this kitchen and see her face staring back at me, but it's not like that."

"It helps you feel closer, right?" I said. "What made you come back?"

"Trish called me. She said you needed my help. I felt so far away from your mom's memory. I didn't know what to do. I'm sorry, Stephen. I shouldn't have left like that." He surveyed the living space. The TV was broken, shards of glass covered the floors and furniture, and all our stuff was scattered on the floor. It looked like someone had robbed us. "Do you remember what happened? Did you see who did this?"

I couldn't get the words out; they were caught in my eyes. He looked at me and saw the truth there, staring back at him.

"Uncle Kasey did this, didn't he? He's been using you and Warren as punching bags! I don't know why your mom thought he could be trusted. I always knew, but she was so sure that he'd changed and that he wouldn't hurt anyone again."

"She did tell you, then."

"Tell me what?" my dad asked, staring at me.

"What he did. What he did to mom when she was a little girl."

"How the hell did you find out about that?" he asked. "Your uncle wouldn't ever admit to something like that."

"That's because nothing fucking happened," Uncle Kasey said. We watched as he stood near the sliding glass door, hidden by the night. He stepped toward us, and my dad helped me off the kitchen floor. "Good to see you, Stu. I didn't think I'd see your face again. The way you ran out of here crying when she died…" He chuckled. It was as if he wasn't really laughing, but taunting. "Not strong enough to take care of your sons. Not even strong enough to stand up to your wife's big brother."

"What is this, Kasey? What the hell did you do to Stephen?" he shouted. But my uncle didn't care. He thought my dad was weak.

"Taught him a fucking lesson," he slurred, curling his lips. "These spoiled brats need some damn discipline. This is my house now. You left, and I did what I had to to keep things in line." He paused to glance at me. "The cops are really on their way now, kid. And they're going to tow your crazy ass away to the asylum."

"What are you talking about? You just beat a fourteen-year-old boy senseless. You really think they're going to arrest Stephen?"

"Your kid's a fucking freak," Uncle Kasey said. "He almost blew up the whole fucking school. He's a nutter, and the whole town's been on a manhunt for him for days. They might even start a riot if the cops don't lock him up fast enough."

"It was an accident," I said. "No one got hurt."

"It doesn't matter," my uncle said. "It's all over now, gimpy." He reached for me, but my dad stood in front of me, protecting me. Uncle Kasey closed in on my dad, trying to intimidate him with his size. My dad wasn't big. He was lean and tall, just like me. He didn't have much muscle mass, and I didn't think he had been in a fist fight in his life. He was a peaceful guy, always kind. But when he stared at my uncle, his eyes were lethal. He hated Uncle Kasey even more than I did.

"You're leaving this house," my dad said, glaring. "If you lay another hand on anyone—man, woman, child— I will personally take your ass out. I know what happened. We all know what you did to Daisy, and she forgave you, but I never will."

Uncle Kasey pushed my dad like they were kids in a schoolyard. "So what? What the fuck are you going to do about it, Stu? You want to hit me? Go right ahead. Show your kid how a man protects his family. Go on!"

"I'm not going to hit you, Kasey. You need help. We're

going to get you into rehab, and with some counseling you might be able to…"

The sentence was left unfinished as my uncle knocked my dad in the jaw. I watched as he prepared to strike again. He curled his fist back like a bed spring, and I saw the metal from the box cutter glint in his hands. He wanted blood. He wanted suffering.

I screamed at my dad to look out as the second blow struck his left side. He backed away and steadied himself from the impact. "He tortured her!" I screamed. "She suffered because of him. She hated herself because of him. We never got all of her, because he stole so much of her from us. You have to beat his ass!"

"Fuck that useless bitch," my uncle spat. "She got what she deserved, and now she's off where she belongs. I won't ever have to hear that annoying fucking voice again." He laughed. "I can still hear her crying, begging me to stop. She was the stupidest, weakest kid you'd ever meet. You should have seen the way she used to jump whenever I got close to her. She was always scared I'd do it again, and I did. I hurt that weak little bitch whenever the fuck I felt like it. She never amounted to nothing. Just like these fucking boys. You should let me raise them, Stu. I might teach them a thing or two about life."

Uncle Kasey stood there taunting, and my dad lunged at him. Their bodies crashed into the wall of cabinets. They struggled, and my dad knocked Uncle Kasey down onto the floor. Blow after blow, he struck my uncle's head. Blood ran down Uncle Kasey's face. He licked his lips, and my dad got off of him.

"Get the fuck out, Kasey," he said. "I don't ever want

to see you again. Or I will report you to the cops. You should hang for what you did."

"I'm untouchable," he laughed, getting up from the ground. "Daisy knew better than to say anything. I would have killed her myself. Too bad the cancer got her first."

My dad screamed, and my uncle lunged at him with the box cutter. My body felt like it was being ripped in two. The pain of everything ripped through me. My uncle had caused my mom to sink so far within herself that she never asked for help. She never told anyone, because he was her brother and her tormentor. I saw her in my mind. I could make out every line in her face as the blinding pain ripped through my chest.

Lightning struck the house.

The little light that lived in my chest jumped out of me and shot right at my uncle. Lightning struck again. Uncle Kasey's body convulsed as the hot light shot through him, and he fell to the floor, unmoving. We waited for him to stir, but he didn't. Warren ran through the back door, and I saw flashing lights rolling down our street. I could hear sirens in the distance.

"Holy shit!" Warren said, gasping for air. "Dad killed Uncle Kasey."

# CHAPTER 21

# LET IT GO

SIRENS WAILED IN my ears. My dad, Warren, and I stared at Uncle Kasey's lifeless body. It convulsed again, and we all stood there, watching. No one wanted to be near him. I edged a bit closer, and he still wore his ridiculous baby grin.

"I think he's really dead," I said. The sounds of sirens grew closer. "The cops are almost here. We can't just leave him like this."

"It's fine," my dad said. "No one killed him. He got struck by lightning."

"I've never seen lightning like that before," Warren said. "That was Stephen's mind control crap. They're going to know it was him. It was the same thing that happened in school."

"What exactly happened in school?" my dad asked. There wasn't a way to explain this to him without him freaking out or calling me crazy. "Someone better tell me what's going on."

"Mom did this," I said, blurting out the first insane thing I could think of. It was an insane thing to say, but I really believed it. "I saw her one night, like a vision of her. There was this tiny glowing orb that jumped down my throat. And it must have been a part of her. Her spirit, or her soul or something, because ever since then, all this strange stuff happens whenever I feel threatened or get near Uncle Kasey." They both stared at me as if I had a second arm growing out from my stomach. "Mom did this. She's been looking out for me the whole time, trying to protect me against Uncle Kasey."

"Stephen," my dad leaned in closer to me. "I miss your mom too. We all do, but it's just not possible. There's no way she'd be able to do anything like that. She's dead."

"I know she's dead," I said.

"No, Dad," Warren interrupted. "I think Stephen's right. I've seen some of this weird stuff go down, and I think he's telling the truth. He gets all possessed-looking whenever that stuff happens. You should have seen the night he smashed Uncle Kasey's beer bottle without even blinking. It came out of nowhere. It had to be her. It had to be Mom."

My dad sighed, leaving his grief to haunt our home. There was a knock at the front door, and my dad walked toward the banging. He opened the door, and three police officers stood on our doorstep.

"Is something wrong?" he asked over the sound of feedback on their pocket radios.

"We're looking for Stephen Wilkes. This is his home, right?"

"Yes, I'm his father. What do you want with Stephen?"

"We have reports from several witnesses that he, and I quote, 'used his mind to destroy school property.' And that came directly from the school principal and a handful of teachers."

"Used his mind? What does that mean?" my dad asked.

"Well, we don't know. He's been missing for days, and we need to take him to the station to get his account of the events."

"He's a minor. This is the most outlandish thing I've ever heard. Look, I know what my son is capable of, and this is the stuff of fairy tales. I can't believe you guys are actually taking this seriously. People can't make things happen with their minds."

"Well, we know that," the shortest cop laughed.

"The point is this," the other cop said. "We have several people claiming that these things happened, and we have to take these kinds of allegations seriously. So it doesn't matter what we think happened. We need to get the facts." He paused and closed his eyes. "Stu, does your son have telepathic powers, yes or no?"

My dad laughed. "Come on, Bill," he said to the cop standing in front. "No, he does not have telepathic powers. But I'm glad you're here. We need an ambulance. Lightning just struck my brother-in-law, and he's not breathing."

One of the cops phoned in a call for an ambulance. "We need to come inside and see Stephen and your brother-in-law, Stu. I'm sorry, but you have to let us in."

"Look, Bill, you've known me for years. Stephen

didn't do anything. This was some kind of freak accident, and people think they saw something they didn't."

"Can we see the boy," Bill said. I walked toward the front door, and my dad stepped aside so the cops could see me. Blood coated my face and ran dry down my shirt. "What the hell happened to him? He's covered in blood! We'll need an ambulance for him too."

"My brother-in-law attacked him."

"The same brother-in-law who was just struck by lightning?" One of the other cops called for back-up. My heart fluttered. Stay calm.

The whole neighborhood was outside in the street. They all stood on their porches or in their yards watching, waiting for drama to ensue. I gripped my chest.

"Yeah," my dad said. "Come on, Bill, you know Kasey Stanford. He's not exactly a stand-up guy. He's been keeping an eye on my boys while I've been away, and as you can see, there's been a lot going on that I didn't know about. I just got home, found him drunk and hitting Stephen. We argued, and then lightning struck him." The short cop was taking notes. "What are you writing?" my dad asked him.

"Stanford?" the short cop asked. "We had to put him in the drunk tank a few weeks ago for starting a fight down at the bar by the steel forge."

"Alright," Bill said. "As soon as the ambulance gets here, everyone is coming with us. We can solve this at the police station."

The ambulance pulled up to our drive, and they put my uncle on a gurney to carry him out. They looked me over and covered a few minor scrapes and bruises. Then they took my uncle's pulse, and there was nothing. He died when the ball of light struck him, but they towed him away nonetheless. The police escorted us away from the house in what felt like slow motion. Everything moved in clipped frames, but my mind was on full speed. I saw Mrs. Way and Elliot walking toward us.

"This is ridiculous," Bethany Way shouted. "You're not actually taking Stephen to jail, Bill. You can't do this. He's just a boy. The whole town's conspiring against him."

They ignored her, and I got into the back seat of the cop car. This was it. I was officially a criminal now. They were going to take me in and force me to use my powers and then what? What would they do to me once they discovered I really was a freak? I needed to think my way out of this. The ambulance drove off, and I tried to use my mind to open the front door to our house, but nothing happened. It didn't budge. I tried to rock my uncle's car back and forth, just as I'd done before, but still nothing happened. The burning in my chest was gone. I thought about my mom, and I felt nothing but a familiar longing for her. It wasn't the same. The little light was finally gone. It must have really gone inside my uncle when lightning struck him.

Elliot's mom and my dad were still outside trying to talk the cops out of hauling me off to jail. "You've got no proof!" Mrs. Way shouted. "Give him a chance to say what happened before you just tow him away. His future is at stake. If you're so convinced he can control things with his mind, then let's see it." She motioned to the crowd of neighbors behind her. "Bring him out here in front of all these people and have him use his powers."

"I don't think that's a good idea, Bethany," my dad interrupted. "We wouldn't want anyone to get hurt."

"You really believe this, Stuart?" she asked. My dad looked away.

Bill stared at my dad, and then he turned to look at me as I sat stone-faced in the backseat of his patrol car. He opened the door. "Get out," he said. "Get out of the car, and let's prove to all these people that nothing happened. I know you didn't do anything, kid. We just need to make them see that small-town gossip is just that—gossip."

I got out of the car. Trish and Liza stood in the very front of the crowd. Trish chewed on her fingernails, while Liza covered her eyes. Bill pulled me in front of the crowd and motioned for the short cop to come toward us. He walked over, and Bill silenced the crowd. Bill grabbed the megaphone from his patrol car so everyone could hear him. The crowd had grown from the folks on our street to nearly the whole damn town.

"Alright, folks," Bill said. "We have in our reports that Stephen used his mind to throw the school principal's body into a line of lockers. So we have Richard here." The short cop waved at the crowd. "And we're going to let Stephen try to move him without touching him."

Bill placed me and Richard across from each other on the sidewalk outside my front yard. I don't know what I was thinking, but I honestly tried to move him. Authority figures intimidated me, and so I felt I had to try. The crowd stayed silent, waiting for something big to happen, but nothing did. I sighed in relief. "You see, folks," Bill's voice sounded on the megaphone, "this was all some kind of coincidence."

"No," a voice shouted from the crowd, and I watched as several people nudged a large boy to the front. It was Jared. "I saw him do it," Jared said. "He broke all the windows in the school. Tell him to break a window!" The crowd jeered in affirmation.

"Fine," Bill groaned into the megaphone. He asked Richard to move me closer to his patrol car. They positioned me in front of it, and again I focused my mind as best I could, but still nothing happened—no glass cracked or shattered. The crowd groaned in disappointment.

"Okay, people," Bill said. "There's clearly been a misunderstanding. This was all just a coincidence, so let's all go home and leave the Wilkes family alone. They've been through enough as it is." The crowd dispersed, and everyone made their way to their homes. "Sorry about that, Stephen," Bill said to me. "And I'm sorry about your mom." And this time the words didn't leave a ringing in my ear.

Trish and Liza walked toward me with their parents beside them. I listened as they gushed over where we'd been and how we'd all run off together. They weren't upset, just glad we were home. It was nice to see Trish and Liza get the attention they deserved from their parents. Liza's mom smiled at her and kissed her hair while she apologized over and over for missing the recital and for not paying her enough attention. I thanked Trish for saving the day by calling my dad. She smiled and let me hug her.

My dad and Warren walked over to me in silence. I hugged my dad again, and he hugged Warren. My family stood by me with Trish and Liza, and I'd never felt so complete. I forgave my dad because I understood him better now. He loved me, and I loved him. We would let go of the past, let go of the hurt. We had to; there wasn't another choice. The sadness that had once choked me had lifted. I still missed my mom, that wouldn't ever change, but I didn't feel alone anymore. My uncle was dead, and the powerlessness I'd clung to had faded with him.

Late that night, as I drifted off to sleep, I could see that strange little light, burning, hanging in the night sky. And I wondered if it had been my mom, keeping me safe, all this time.

# ACKNOWLEDGMENTS

Stephen's story came to me in a dream, and I never would have had the courage to write this book had it not been for the guidance and support of mentors, friends, and loved ones. I want to thank my mother for always thinking the world of me, my best friend, Sara Roth, for listening to my tripe and reading all of my terrible drafts, and a special thank you to my editor, Emma Simmons, for sifting through this book with a fine-toothed comb. To everyone who believed in me and offered words of support, thank you. I am not brave, I am not bold, but I'm always willing to try, and I hope that the readers of this book will learn that you should always do your best even when you're at your worst.

# ABOUT THE AUTHOR

Kris Villarreal is a literary fiction and fantasy author living in Atlanta. She was born in 1988 outside San Francisco and raised by parents of Mexican, French, and African- American descent. She graduated from the University of Georgia with a degree in Journalism and another in Women's Studies. With a background in editing and a love for literature, Kris pursued her dream of writing fiction early in her career. She finds comfort in crafting stories that focus on societal ills with themes of fantasy and magical realism. Kris loves anime, tea, books of all kinds, and studying languages. Her debut novel Logost was released in July 2014.